BLACK
PLATINUM

In the Shadows

BOOK 6

Talia and Sebastian

a billionaire SEAL story

BLACK
PLATINUM

In the Shadows
BOOK 6
Talia and Sebastian

by P.T. MICHELLE

ISBN-10: 1939672368
ISBN-13: 9781939672360

Interior designed and formatted by E.M. Tippetts Book Designs
www.emtippettsbookdesigns.com

Cover by P.T. Michelle and Najla Qamber

To stay informed when the next **P.T. Michelle** book will be released, join P.T. Michelle's free newsletter http://bit.ly/11tqAQN

BLACK PLATINUM

In the Shadows

BOOK 6

Talia and Sebastian

by P.T. MICHELLE

You are cordially invited…

When wedding plans go awry and tragedy hits, Sebastian and Talia race against time to uncover the culprit who dared to strike out at the Blakes.

While wading through murky family waters to discover the truth, Mister Black and Little Red's relationship deepens and simmers to new levels.

Author's Note: BLACK PLATINUM can be read as a standalone story, but for the richest reading experience you can always start with the first book, MISTER BLACK, to see how Sebastian and Talia's epic love story began.

In The Shadows Series :

AVAILABLE NOW...

Mister Black (1) (Sebastian & Talia Part 1, Novella)

Scarlett Red (2) (Sebastian & Talia Part 2, Novel)

Blackest Red (3) (Sebastian & Talia Part 3, Novel)

Gold Shimmer (4) (Cass & Calder Part 1, Novel)

Steel Rush (5) (Cass & Calder Part 2, Novel)

Black Platinum (6) (Sebastian & Talia, Novel)

COMING UP...

Reddest Black (7) (Sebastian & Talia, Novel) - October 2017

CHAPTER ONE

Sebastian

Whoever said marriage is boring has never been married to Talia. I roll my head from one shoulder to the other to relieve my frustration before I push open BLACK Security's main door. At least work should keep me sane over the next couple of days.

"Good morning, Bash," Calder calls out with a wide grin as he pours himself a cup of coffee.

"Maybe *yours* was," I grate, while mentally reminding myself to pay Cass back for convincing Talia that we should "officially" marry in a church so friends and family can celebrate. Since when did celibacy become part of this re-marry package deal? *Fuck that.* Just because it was only Talia, me, and a judge the first time around doesn't negate the promises we made, "'til death do us part" included.

When Calder's eyes alight with knowing amusement over the top of his mug, I snap, "And tell your fiancé she's officially on my shit list," before I slam my office door.

Talia can claim being traditional and call it "bad luck to see each other until the wedding" all she wants, but that just means my bed is fucking empty. One night without her and I'm ready to bust someone's balls or punch a wall this morning, whichever comes first.

To add insult to injury, my loving wife refused to tell me where she's staying for the next couple of nights until the wedding. She agreed to let BLACK Security's best guy shadow her, but then made me promise that I wouldn't try to find out from Theo where she went. Needless to say the tight-lipped bastard definitely won't be getting a bonus this year.

Unbuttoning my suit jacket, I settle in my chair and turn on my laptop. I thrum my fingers impatiently on the mahogany desk, pissed at how long it's taking to boot up. Apparently even going for a five-mile run before dawn did nothing to ease the tension building inside me.

I swivel toward the window and pull out my phone, punching out a text to Talia.

That bed must've seemed massive last night.

I totally starfished it!

She sounds entirely too content.

Tell me where you're staying and I'll come keep you warm tonight.

Nice try. I stayed toasty all night long.

Grumbling my annoyance, I shoot back a reply.

You know you missed falling asleep completely worn out.

Who says I wasn't completely worn out?

I clench my jaw until it feels like my teeth are going to crack.

Don't push me, Little Red.

But isn't that what I do best, Mister Black?

I picture her tilting her head and tucking a strand of her red hair behind her ear, a sexy, challenging smile on her kissable lips and shake my head.

Every damn day, sweetheart.

I love you, too. Just two more nights and I'm all yours.

You're already all mine. No religious ritual can seal that deal better than you calling my name over and over until you beg me to stop.

Such arrogance!

Do you need a reminder why I'm your Rainbow Master? I'm going to enjoy painting that sweet ass a gorgeous shade of crimson.

Gah...go to work!

All it took was some early morning banter to stave off the edginess riding me, but at least now I can concentrate. Smirking, I tuck my phone away and pull up BLACK Security's updated list of case files on my laptop before buzzing Calder's phone. "Get your ass in here so we can discuss the week."

A few seconds later, my cousin and business partner opens the door, eyebrow hiked. "Are you done biting my head off?"

"Are you still alive?"

With a deep chuckle he slides into the leather chair in front of my desk and takes a sip of his coffee. "It's just two more days, Bash. Chill."

My fingers pause over the keyboard. "I wouldn't be so glib. You're going to be in my shoes soon enough."

"Cass isn't traditional at all," Calder says, snorting.

I meet his stare with a bold one. "I'll bet you a thousand bucks Cass is more traditional than you think."

Calder's gaze narrows. "I think I know my fiancé far better than you."

"Are you taking the bet or not?"

"Hell yeah. I like easy money, but let's make this interesting," he says, setting his cup down on the edge of my desk. "If I win, I get your office."

"What's wrong with your office?"

He gestures to the window behind me. "Yours has a better view."

I grunt and shake my head. "It's a moot point. You're going to lose. *When* I win, the next time Cass has an idea that involves taking my wife away from me for even one night, you'll nip that shit in the bud. Got it?"

Calder grins and leans back, folding his arms. "You're on."

"If Cass so much as utters the word 'traditional' in relation to any aspect of your wedding, you've lost the bet," I say just as he picks his mug back up.

"Hey, that's too fucking broad."

"And *that's* why I'm CEO." I flash a ruthless smile and hit the enter button. "Grab your copy from the printer and let's discuss upcoming team assignments."

Calder and I spend the next two hours reading over new contracts, determining if we have enough staff to cover the clients' needs or if a personnel expansion is necessary.

While debating the finer points of personality meshing verses skill level, a phone call from my father stops me mid-sentence. Adam Blake rarely calls. Definitely not during work hours. What does my father want? I pick up my phone. "Is everything okay with Mina and Josi?"

"Your sister and her daughter are fine, Sebastian. I'm calling about another matter. Why did you give my bodyguard an assignment without my authorization? Just because I asked you to come work for Blake Industries doesn't give you rights to my employees."

"BLACK Security keeps me busy enough. What are you talking about? I didn't assign Den to any detail—"

I flick a gaze Calder's way just to confirm and he quickly shakes his head, his brow furrowed.

"Den said it was a BLACK Security assignment, son."

"Hold on…" Still annoyed by my father's accusation,

I stand and open my door, ready to call out to the cubicle bullpen and clear up the misunderstanding when my gaze lands on Theo sitting at his desk, one-punching his meaty fingers on his keyboard. "I'll call you back."

"Don't you dare hang up on me—"

Clicking off, I stalk toward Theo and yank the headphones off his head. "What the ever-loving-fuck are you doing here, Connelly?"

His thick light brown eyebrows pull together as he slowly folds muscular arms against his barrel chest. "Whoever you're pissed at, don't drag me into it."

"I'm looking at him!" I bellow. "You're supposed to be watching Talia."

"Your memory is apparently going." Theo's new buzz cut shifts forward with his frown. "You're the one who told that British fellow to send me home."

"What exactly did Den say to you?"

"He said, 'Mr. Blake asked me to take over Talia's guard duty. Head back to the office.'"

That sneaky sonofabitch. I take a steadying breath and grit out, "Den works for my *father*, Theo."

"But he said, 'Mr. Blake...'" Theo trails off, his face going pale. "Well, shit!"

When he starts to stand, I put my hand on his shoulder and hand him his headphones back. "No, I'll deal with this personally. In the future, unless the order comes directly from me, ignore the hell out of it. Are we clear?"

"Understood." Theo rubs his hand against the back of his neck and sighs. "I'm sorry, Bash. But with Den's military intelligence skills and massive size, at least you know Talia's more than covered."

"The point is, she should never *need* someone like Den backing her up," I growl before pivoting for the door.

"You want me with you?" Calder calls after me just as I pull the main door open, my phone to my ear.

Of course my wife's phone goes straight to voicemail. I glance his way. "I need you to coordinate here. Have Elijah ping Talia's phone and Den's too, then send me the info."

When Talia's voicemail beeps as I'm getting into my car, I slam the door and speak calmly into my phone, "All bets are off, Little Red. You don't get to smoke-and-mirror your husband with traditional wedding ritual BS, then expect him not to come after you. Whatever assignment you felt you needed Den for, can't be *safe*."

Calder calls as I pull into Tribune's parking lot. Even though I called Talia's assistant, I don't feel any better when I see my wife's car sitting in the lot. I hit the speaker button and my cousin's voice fills my car. "Both Talia's and Den's cell phones must be turned off. We can't get a signal for either one."

"Talia's assistant says she's out on an assignment. I'm here at the Tribune. I'll find out what the deal is."

Before I hang up, Calder says, "I called Cass to see if she knew where Talia might be. She didn't have a clue—"

"Why are you telling me this?"

"Shut up and just listen. After I explained what was going on, Cass asked me to remind you that storming into Talia's boss's office is probably the worst thing you could do two days before your wedding—"

"We're already married," I grit out, annoyed.

"Do you still *want* to be?"

Exhaling harshly, I lean my head back against the leather seat and close my eyes. Talia worked hard to regain the Tribune's respect after some bad information put her investigative story and reputation at risk in the past. This was her second time working for the newspaper and the last thing I'd ever want to do is jeopardize a career she worked so hard to get back on track. When I asked her to marry me, I promised I would protect her, but that I wouldn't smother her. I want her to be happy, for her career to flourish. *Fuck, this is harder than I thought it would be.* "Fine. I won't go into the building."

"Also, I thought you should know that Elijah's daily news scan just caught the Blake name in a special on-line edition this morning. It's your engagement announcement. I know you wouldn't send an announcement out there—"

"Hell no!" I cut him off and quickly pull the article up on my phone. I scan the picture of Talia and me, irritation rising. "This has Isabel's fingerprints all over it. She'll do anything for more Blake family limelight, despite the fact she can't stand me."

"Yeah, I wouldn't put this past your stepmother. Get ready for a write up in tomorrow's paper and to be hounded by the paparazzi at the rehearsal. I'm sure Talia will touch base later. She knows sending Theo here would alert you. Are you coming back to the office?"

Of course she knows. I narrow my gaze on my wife's car. There's only so much patience she can expect from someone with my protective nature. "I'll be in later."

CHAPTER TWO

Talia

"*Who* is that?" Nathan says as he pulls his car up behind Den's in front of a house on the Lower East Side.

I take in Den's impeccable suit stretched across folded arms as he casually leans against his BMW in eighty-degree June heat. He's as unruffled as if it's a cool sixty. With broad shoulders and towering height, he's so impressively intimidating that he'd drawn a few young guys onto their front porch, but no one had apparently dared to approach the six-foot-five stranger hanging out in front of their house. Den didn't hesitate once I called and told him I needed someone to back me up while visiting a sketchy neighborhood. He instantly asked if he could drive me, but I told him I'd meet him here instead.

I nod toward Den. "He's the associate I mentioned

would meet us."

Nathan cuts the engine and runs his hand nervously through his short dirty-blond curls. "He certainly leaves an impression. I guess your *husband* was too busy to fill in."

I ignore my ex's dig about Sebastian and address his first comment. "See, I told you that you didn't need to come," I murmur, then grin my appreciation at Den as he opens the car door before I get a chance to. "Thank you, Den. I appreciate you meeting us here."

"It's my pleasure, Miss Tal—"

"Just Talia," I say, reminding him I don't stand on formality. Closing my door, I gesture to Nathan emerging from the other side of his car. "Den, this is a work colleague, Nathan."

"You're British?" Nathan doesn't bother to hide his surprise as he closes his door and beeps his key fob.

"I'm Kenyan and Irish, but I was raised in London."

"He's also ex-MI6, so mind your manners." I wave my finger at Nathan in a mock-stern tone.

As we approach the house, a thinner guy, about five-nine in height, with spiked dark hair and equally dark eyes, separates from the group. Tucking his hands into his baggy jeans' pockets, he says, "Are you Talia Murphy?"

I nod and gesture to Nathan and Den. "These are my colleagues. And you are?"

"I'm Paulo." The guy eyes Den warily. "You said

there would be two of you when you set this up. Banks doesn't like surprises. Only two can meet with him for the interview."

Den steps forward. "I go where she goes."

"That's fine." I quickly wave toward Nathan. "Nathan can wait out here."

Nathan glances at the digital camera he carried from the car. "But I'm here to take pictures."

I lift the camera from his hand. "I can take the shots. Banks is giving an exclusive interview. We need to play by his rules."

Paulo nods his approval and opens the door to lead the way into the house.

"As you wish, Mrs. Blake," Nathan says.

Lately, Nathan has started using my new last name whenever he's annoyed with me. Just as I clench my teeth to keep from snapping at him, Paulo stops walking and turns around, suspicion in his eyes. "Blake? I thought you said your name was Murphy?"

"Murphy is my maiden and professional name on my Tribune articles. Blake is my married name."

"Blake?" A booming voice interrupts just as a bald bull-of-a-man walks up, the wood floor shaking with his heavy-footed approach. He sweeps a calculating gaze over Den's attire, then rubs his dark goatee. "With that suit and BMW...as in *the* Blakes?"

The last thing I expected was to drag Sebastian's family

into this interview. "Yes, *those* Blakes." Putting my hand out, I step forward. "Talia Murphy. It's nice to meet you, Mr. Banks."

"Banks, no 'mister,'" he corrects. Ignoring my hand, he folds his arms over his thick chest and equally thick middle. The scar slicing across half his face stands out as his brown eyes give me a guarded once over. "Which Blake are you hitched to?"

He's entirely too interested in my last name. Lowering my hand, I slide a gaze Den's way. I need to refocus the discussion back to Banks. While we talked on the phone, that's all he cared about. "Thank you for agreeing to do the interview. Once I learned about the good your crew has done overall for your neighborhood in keeping it safe, including adding lights and rebuilding bleachers at the local park, and the new donation center in that old church, I wanted to give you the spotlight you deserve."

"I want to know who's asking the questions, so I'll ask you again..." he says in a harsher tone. "Which Blake are you married to, Mrs. *Blake*?"

He's not going to let this go. "I'm married to the oldest son, Sebastian."

"Well, well." Banks tenses and gives me a once over from head-to-toe. "The stubborn bastard did well for himself with such a fine looking wife."

"And *wow*, she has a brain too." When Banks's brown eyes narrow, I instantly regret not tempering my sarcastic response, but the fact he somehow knows Sebastian throws me off my game. *How are they connected?*

Before I can apologize, Banks snorts. "He was just as mouthy."

"You know my husband?"

"Yeah, we know Blackie," Paulo cuts in as he moves to stand beside Banks.

"Or knew, rather," Banks finishes, gesturing for me to follow him into the living room. "You can interview me in here."

Blackie. That name was from Sebastian's teenage years before he moved in with his father and away from the Lower East Side. I glance across the room to the men of various ages sitting around watching TV and playing video games on the leather couch. The way they're flicking their gazes between Banks and me with a wary gleam in their eyes, I can't help but wonder in what capacity Sebastian knew Banks and his crew. Was he part of this group in his youth? He told me once that a gang tried to recruit him and he had to fight to remain independent.

As far as I can tell, these guys don't appear to be openly carrying guns. That's why I wanted to interview their leader. He'd managed to keep his neighborhood safe without using gun violence. I didn't see a single firearm tucked in any of their waistlines. But now that I know Sebastian had some kind of connection to them, I'm really glad I didn't let Theo attend this interview. There's no way he wouldn't report this back to my husband. And being the private man that he is...I think Sebastian wouldn't want the past he left behind resurfacing. I'm more than relieved that Banks has decided to move on to the interview.

Shooing the men off the sofa, the leader barks, "Go outside for a while," then gestures for me to sit. While Paulo moves over to stand next to the big window near the front door, his gaze never leaving Nathan on the porch, Banks glares at Den. Holding Bank's gaze, Den moves to the back of the sofa, positioning himself directly behind me.

"Why do you want to do this interview?" Banks gives up his staring contest with Den and parks his thick bulk on the coffee table in front of me.

I realize he's sitting close and putting himself in a higher position on purpose, but I keep my response even this time. He didn't get to where he is without asserting authority. "Normally I do investigative pieces for the Tribune, but when I learned about your group, I was intrigued. I know that the police have rousted the Banks's Boys a few times over the last decade or so, but overall you all have remained unscathed, while your neighborhood is known to be one of the safest. The dynamic sounded interesting and an overall positive success story, which sadly doesn't often get highlighted in this area."

"You see this face?" He points to his scar. "This is the face of someone who sticks his neck out, dives into danger and eats it for lunch. That's what being part of my crew means. We look out for each other, just like we look out for the hood. Many of the guys here don't have anyone else. We are family." Lifting his chin toward me, he continues. "What would you know about any of that? How can you possibly know what does or doesn't go on in this area of town sitting in your cushy Tribune office?"

"Are you interviewing me?" I ask, tilting my head.

Hooking his booted foot across his other knee, Banks folds gold-ringed fingers around his ankle. "Just trying to understand your angle."

From the high-end video games/TVs and brand new leather furniture, Banks and his "boys" have money coming from some source, but I know it's not drugs or guns. Am I curious about that piece? Sure. The downside of investigative journalism is that you're always looking to uncover the bad stuff so you can make your story stand out in the sensationalism noise among all the other headlines. But even a paper as investigation heavy as the Tribune needs some balance, so every so often we'll highlight the positive side of a story.

Banks is my story.

I flip open my notepad and retrieve a pen from its spiral. "No angle, Banks. I'm doing what I said, highlighting the positive. I want to talk about better police stats and lower gun violence in your neighborhood, and discuss how your group works with the community center's youth program, helping with projects that directly benefit them, like adding more lights to the local park and building new bleachers. And for the record, I know what it's like to live in fear of someone with power over you, to not know how you're going to pay your rent, let alone buy your next meal. I've lost everything, including family, and had to start all over, so yeah…I think I'm qualified to do this interview. Does that satisfy your need to know if I'll write my article from a point of understanding?"

Banks rests his elbows on his knees, a slow grin spreading on his face. "Ask away, lady reporter. Some things I'll answer, some I won't, due to protecting my neighborhood and all."

Nodding, I lift the camera. "Can I take a couple of pictures to go with the interview?"

He rubs his goatee, then folds his arms across his chest. Jutting his chin at a tough-guy angle, his dark eyes shine. "Have at it."

When the interview is over and Den and I walk out of the house, I give Nathan an apologetic smile. "I'm sorry you had to wait out here."

Buttoning his collar back up and tightening his loosened tie, Nathan rubs the sweat off his temple and grumbles, "Did you get a couple of pictures?"

I nod and hand him his camera back. "Can you email them to me?"

"Sure. You ready to head back?"

"I'll drop Talia off at the Tribune," Den says before I can answer.

After Den closes the passenger car door behind me and then climbs into the driver side, I wait until we pull away to speak. "Thank you for coming on such short notice. Banks called at the last minute. He only agreed to the interview if I could do it today." When he raises his eyebrow, I can read the question in his gaze. He was too polite to ask in front of Nathan. "Yes, my husband could've backed me up, but I'm trying hard to stick to the tradition of not seeing him before the rehearsal dinner and our wedding."

Den nods his understanding, then glances my way after he turns out of the neighborhood. "What did you think of Banks's interest in Sebastian?"

"They definitely had a past, it seems. But I'm glad Banks let it go once he decided that I didn't have any other agenda behind why I was here."

"Based on the undertones in Banks's statements, Sebastian wouldn't have been happy with this meeting, Talia."

"I know that now." I meet his light brown gaze. The striking contrast against his dark skin never ceases to warrant a moment of appreciation. "Sebastian really hasn't discussed much about his past life in the Lower East Side with me. And I get it. There are some things we'd rather leave behind."

"Until the past and present cross paths," Den muses.

"What's done is done," I say on a sigh. "Banks was certainly interesting to interview. Can you believe that all of the guys are pretty much orphans of some sort? Talk about a unique way to be raised."

"Without family it makes sense they would gravitate to someone who could look after them. I noticed you didn't drill Banks too deeply as to how they earn a living. Since when does 'odd jobs here and there' earn enough to afford high end TVs and furniture?"

"Is that your former agent skills kicking in?" I tease, wondering about Den's life with the MI6. *Why did he leave?*

He flicks on his blinker and glances back to the road, but not before I see a flash of perfect teeth with his quick smile. "Just as I noticed your sharp investigative skills taking a back seat during this interview."

"Yep, but I made Banks a promise that this would only be about the good his group has done and I'm sticking to it. Please do me a favor and don't disclose where we've been if Sebastian asks. He'll learn about it when the article comes out the day after our wedding. By then, he'll see that the interview was just a feel good piece and nothing more."

Turning onto the road that leads to my office, Den says, "My career *is* discretion. I'm not about to change that now."

"The last thing I want Sebastian to think is that I was

out digging up dirt on his past right before our wedding. Yes, discovering their connection was a heck of a fluke, but I'll just write my article and move on."

"Don't worry, Talia. My discretion remains unchanged. Never hesitate to call. I look forward to our...adventures."

"Thank you, Den. I value your friendship on top of your professional skills."

He slides his gaze to me as he slows to a stoplight near the Tribune's office building. "I no longer see pain and sadness in your eyes now that you're with Sebastian. I'll help in any way I can to keep that from happening."

"Because you know what that feels like?" I ask, tilting my head to see his response.

"Some sad memories we keep for a reason," he says, nodding slowly. "The pain they evoke only fades in the background."

The memory of little Amelia comes to mind. I miss her sweet smile and tight arms squeezing my neck. I instantly reach up to touch my locket that holds the only memory I have of her—the "two Lias drawing" locked inside. "Is it 'one day' yet?" I ask Den, referring to his promise to tell me about his past.

"I have also lost," is all he says before turning into the Tribune.

I notice the flash of pain his vague comment causes. I want to ask more, but I don't get a chance to respond before he gets out and comes around my side of the car, opening my door. "I believe you have an interview to write up, Mrs. Blake."

It took the rest of the day to compile Banks's answers to my questions and write my article. I wanted it to be balanced and thorough while holding onto my promise to Banks. I submitted it to my boss, Stan, just before the end of the day. I leave the office and just as I slow to a stop at the red light outside the Tribune, I realize I'd been so immersed in work that I'd forgotten to turn my phone back on. The moment the screen flares to life, a missed voicemail from Sebastian instantly pops up and my heart trips. He never leaves voicemails. Instead, he prefers the back and forth banter texting allows.

Since I'm not far from my father's bookstore, I quickly head in that direction for a place to park and listen to Sebastian's message. I finally find a space down the street, then cut the engine and hit the play button on my phone. My accomplished mood for the day instantly flat-lines at the anger in my husband's voice. For some reason he's got it in his head that the time we're spending apart before the wedding was just so I could keep him in the dark about an assignment. *Ugh, I could've handled this better.* Now I'm especially glad the article won't release until after the wedding. I've been avoiding direct phone calls since yesterday so my husband couldn't use his supreme seductive prowess to convince me to come home, but

I know only a phone call will fix this. I start to dial his number when a commotion at the entrance of my father's bookstore draws my attention.

My father is holding his bookstore door open and gesturing angrily after my Aunt Vanessa as she walks out. My heart jerks and my hand instantly curls tight around my phone. Despite her attempts to try and contact me, I haven't seen or talked to my aunt since I discovered her role in ending my engagement to Nathan. While she was right that I would've been miserable with him, that wasn't her call to make.

But I've also struggled with the fact she didn't stop my mother from committing suicide when she knew she was unwell, and that she left me in a vulnerable situation as a young teen while she worked crazy hours. Deep down a part of me wants to believe that my aunt does love me, but her skewed viewpoint in how she shows that worries me. And now she's here talking—actually *arguing*—with my father? My relationship with Kenneth McAdams only began this year. We're just getting to know each other. If my aunt is trying to manipulate that too, I won't struggle any longer with my guilt in staying away from her.

They exchange a few more words and then my aunt walks to her car. I wait until she leaves before I walk over to the bookshop.

"Talia! Come in, come in." My dad gestures the moment I walk inside, the frown on his lined face instantly morphing into a broad smile. Pushing a cart of books over next to the register, he turns to a blonde woman about ten years or so older than me standing behind the desk. "Simone, the register is doing that funky thing again. Can you fix it? And when you're done, could you please lock up and take care of shelving these books from the kids' corner? I need to talk to my daughter."

"Sure thing, Kenneth," she says, pulling the cart full of books forward.

"Hi, Simone, I'm Talia." Glancing at my dad, I grin. "Business must be picking up."

He nods. "I learned so much standing in line at your book signing, listening to your fans chat about books and how they discovered them, that I decided to try targeted advertising on social media. Yep, advertising is my new best friend. With the extra customers I've brought into the store, I was able to hire Simone." He gestures to Simone, smiling. "Turns out, she not only loves books, but she's also a whiz with computers too."

"Thanks for helping," I say to Simone as my father hooks his arm in mine and tugs me toward a door at the back of the store.

She turns a steady gaze my way, offering a quick smile. "It's nice to meet you, Talia. Don't worry about the register, I've got it covered," she calls after us as my father opens the door to his office.

The moment he shuts the door and gestures to the

cushioned chair in front of his desk, I sit and lift my gaze to his green one that's so like mine. "What was that yelling contest I just witnessed at the entrance of your store? Why in the world was my aunt here?"

Kenneth perches on the edge of the desk facing me. "This is the second time she has come by. The first time was a couple weeks ago. I was civil and treated her like any other customer. She didn't mention you at all. Instead before she left, she just said she was glad that I'd figured out my life."

"Talk about a backhanded compliment," I murmur, shaking my head.

He shrugs and adjusts the collar of his light gray sweater over the navy collared shirt underneath. "She's not incorrect. It took me a while to get my head on straight."

"She was probably just curious, but why did she come back?"

He slides a hand in his black dress pant pocket and shakes his head. "She walked around and pretended to look at books, but then made a beeline for me as soon as I was done helping a customer. She asked me point blank if I was going to walk you down the aisle."

"What?" I blink rapidly. "How does she even know about the wedding?"

"You obviously haven't read today's news." My father chuckles as he lifts a print out from his desk and hands it to me. "A special edition went out on-line. I'm sure it'll be splashed all over the other papers tomorrow. It's big news around here when a Blake gets married, you know."

I stare at the article from the society section announcing our upcoming wedding. The accompanying picture is one Mina had taken just last weekend. Sebastian is wrapping his arms around my waist as we stand on our patio at our house in the Hamptons. It's a lovely picture. We look happy, but it's also a personal moment of laughter among family. Between his BLACK Security business with elite clients all over the city and beyond, and his background as a Navy SEAL, the man I love covets his privacy. Even our apartment is unlisted. But if my ex saw this article this morning, now I know why Nathan was extra snarky today. *Ugh.*

I gape at my father. "I have no idea how this happened. Sebastian would never do this."

My father points to the paper. "That's how your aunt found out that you're getting married. She insisted that I help you two reconcile. She wants to be invited and went on and on about how she's the one who raised you, not me. Needless to say, I didn't bother telling her you're already married. She was getting loud enough as it was, drawing curious gazes from patrons. I don't want or need my past waved around, so I finally had to ask her to leave, which she didn't appreciate. Hence the drama as she left."

My heart twists with guilt. I've carried an invitation for my aunt in my purse for a week now. Plaguing doubt kept me from mailing it. My father will never know all the gritty details her past transgressions caused in my life, but he knows enough. "I'm sorry you got caught up in the middle of this."

Kenneth folds his arms and nods toward the paper. "I take it you had a busy day to miss that kind of news?"

I start to speak, then it hits me and I chuckle. "My very private husband must also not know about this news, or I most definitely would've heard about it from him. I guess you could say we've uh…been living in a bubble the last twenty-four hours."

His eyebrows shoot up. "Is this good or bad news?"

I shrug. "Sebastian will hate that it was announced to the world with the heat of a thousand suns, but there's nothing we can do about it now. I'm sorry Aunt Vanessa harassed you. After the way she left, I have a feeling she won't be back."

"So…are you going to invite her?"

I'm so surprised by his question, I stare at him for a couple seconds before I reply. "Are you serious? After what just happened here and the things I've told you she's responsible for?"

Nodding, he sits in the chair across from me and clasps one of my hands between his. "Talia, I'm not a perfect man. I've made mistakes in my past. Leaving you and your mother was the biggest one, and I'll have to live with missing out on your childhood forever because of it. It would be hypocritical of me not to encourage you to consider inviting Vanessa." I start to speak, but he interrupts. "Let me finish. You don't have to forgive her or let her back into your life, but I can tell that she sincerely loves you and it would be a gesture of goodwill on your part to let the woman who raised you see you get married."

He cups my cheek with one hand, his eyes turning glassy. "If you hadn't given me a chance to get to know you, we wouldn't have a relationship. You and Vanessa may never be as close as you once were, but I'm a firm believer in second chances with all the cards on the table, eyes wide open...whatever the metaphor."

I lay my hand over his and squeeze. "I'll think about it."

Releasing my face, he smiles and clasps my hands once more. "Vanessa had an excellent question, but I honestly didn't know the answer. Are you walking yourself down the aisle, young lady?"

Emotion wells and I sniff back tears. "I would love it if you would walk me down the aisle, but I wasn't sure how to ask you."

"I'd be honored." A huge smile spreads across his face, a hint of color riding his cheeks. "And now I'll need a tux."

"That won't be necessary. A nice suit will suffice."

"Not for this honor it won't!" He releases me, eyes alight with excitement. "Well, I've got to get busy. I have a friend who owns a shop, but that means I'll need to go see him tonight to get fitted."

Nodding, I stand. "Okay then, I'll head out. Are we still on next month at Andres?"

"I'd never miss a lunch with my Tally-girl." I can't help but smile at the sweet nickname, but when I start to walk out of his office, he says, "And Talia?"

When I turn back, kind eyes hold mine. "Definitely think about that second chance. Everyone makes mistakes. It's how they rectify them that says the most about their character."

CHAPTER THREE

Talia

I mull my father's suggestion about Aunt Vanessa the whole way back to my apartment. It's not that I'm not a forgiving soul, but she has already ruined one relationship. I might be thankful that I didn't marry Nathan, but I don't want anything to mess with what Sebastian and I have. I love that man so much my heart twists whenever I think of him. I was lonely sleeping without him last night, but he's so strong and domineering, if I don't keep him on his toes and match him wit for wit, a tiny part of me worries that after such a turbulent relationship, now that we're married, he might grow bored.

Once I settle in for the evening, I'll call and talk to him about today's misunderstanding. I'm just glad that Cass has taken on handling all the wedding arrangements. My best friend is going above and beyond with her maid-of-honor duties. She says she considers it training for her upcoming wedding, but between today's unexpected surprises with Banks and then my aunt, I don't think I can handle wedding mishaps on top of everything else. I'm relieved I let her take the reins.

As I reach into my purse for the apartment key, I pause and slide my fingers over the red silk I purchased for a wedding gift for Sebastian on my lunch hour today. The moment my gaze landed on the silk, the striking color sold me. I had to buy more than I needed since the merchant only sold it in small bolts, but I've been searching for just the right color to have a tie made for my husband and I wasn't passing it up. Sebastian already has a bluish-red tie, but this one will be much brighter.

It's bold…just like my husband.

My phone beeps with an incoming message from Cass and I grab my cell from my purse, wishing my best friend was actually sitting in our old apartment right now instead of living at Calder's house. We could curl up on the couch and eat an entire carton of ice cream while chatting about the irresistible but sometimes infuriating men in our lives.

Smiling at the appealing thought, I click to read her message.

Great pic on-line, but between that surprise wedding announcement, then you ditching your detail today…GIRL, what were you thinking? You know your husband won't be thrilled.

I quickly text her back.

I didn't put that picture out there. I guess that means I can scratch YOU off my "you're so dead list"! Mina's next. And yeah, I really screwed my security up! Sebastian thinks I smoke-screened him, and that even this pre-wedding time we're spending apart is just a ruse to keep him in the dark about an assignment.

She immediately responds.

Ugh, that sucks! Let's get together and chat over drinks. I need to go over wedding stuff with you. Calder and I have a quick errand to run, but I can meet you at six-thirty at Fine Tapas.

Please don't let there be any hiccups with wedding stuff. I bite my lip and tap out a response.

Sounds good. Thank you for keeping me sane. See you in a little bit.

Sending that message, I dash off a quick text to Sebastian.

No smoke screen. I had to go to an area of town that Den was familiar with. My client couldn't come to me and I didn't have time to debate with Theo. Everything went fine. I'll call you in five minutes.

My phone rings just as I start to drop it into my purse. Assuming it's my husband, I quickly answer. "Hey."

But when no one says anything and then a hang-up click echoes in my ear, I glance at the Caller ID. Blocked call. That's the second time in two days. It's probably my aunt. I'll call her tomorrow. I just can't deal with trying to talk to her right now.

Sighing, I drop my phone into my purse, then grab my key and walk into the apartment. I've got forty minutes to change into jeans before I have to meet Cass. The moment I shut the door, instant darkness surrounds me. *Ugh*, I guess the streetlight outside finally blew. It was flickering last night.

With a sigh, I carefully take the couple of steps toward the couch table. Setting my purse on it, I dig blindly into its cavernous depths, pushing past my sunglasses case, hairbrush, checkbook, and notepad while groping for my phone so I can light my way to the lamp next to the side chair.

The barest sound of movement hits me just before masculine cologne assails my senses.

"Sebastian…" I exhale his name in a gasping, breathy whisper as he pulls my hips back. My dress' thin material may as well be tissue against his hard erection imprinting on my ass.

"I can't decide which to make you pay for first: convincing me you truly believed we shouldn't see each other before the wedding rehearsal, or the fact I didn't sleep at all last night," his voice rumbles in my ear. "Either way…" Strong hands fold tighter around my hips in a firm grip. "This sweet ass of yours is toast." Hot lips sear against the side of my throat, his fingers gripping me tighter. "I expect to hear you saying my name like that several times tonight."

I clutch my purse's straps to keep from reaching back and digging my fingers into his hair and pulling him closer. "I planned to call you. I'm sorry for the misunderstanding earlier today, but you're not supposed to see me until rehearsal. You promised."

"Like you promised to let Theo watch over you until then?" he says in an edgy tone.

His deep voice and the sandalwood notes of his cologne are both comforting and arousing. I want to melt against him. I miss him too, which scares me how my happiness is directly tied to his strong presence in my life. I've become addicted to being challenged on so many levels with him. "I *promised* to let a detail shadow me, which I did."

"Are you really playing the 'fine print' card?" His hands tighten on my body and his mouth moves to my ear, his tone unrelenting. "If you needed Den, then fuck promises and traditional bullshit. You should've called *me*." He slides a hand to my stomach pushing me back against him, his tone softening. "You make it hard to keep my word, Little Red, but technically, I still am. I can't *see* you."

His voice is husky, yet tense. Even though he's angry with me, he still wants me. God this is hard. I want him just as much. "Now who's working the fine details?" I say, letting amusement bleed into my comment. "How did you find me?"

"When it comes to you, I'll always be ruthless and unrelenting, taking every advantage." He presses closer, his deep voice rumbling against my back.

As I realize that he deftly avoided answering my question, familiar voices just outside the apartment door send me into action. I grab my purse and tug Sebastian's arm, whispering, "Hurry, follow me."

The moment we stumble into the tiny bathroom and I quickly close the door, pressing my ear against it, my husband rests his hand at the base of my spine, his deep voice sliding along my skin like a lover's caress. "This is new."

"Hold on," I quickly say as Cass and Calder enter the apartment talking. By their discussion, they're apparently here to take the new coffee table she'd bought a few months ago. She's asking Calder to carry it over to the house while she meets up with me for drinks.

A couple seconds pass before Sebastian speaks next to my ear, "Why the hell are we hiding in the bathroom from Cass and Calder?"

"Whisper," I insist as I turn to face him, pressing my back against the door. "Cass is convinced that we can't last three days apart." It's hard not to react when he slides his thumb enticingly down my cheekbone.

"She's right. Come home, Little Red."

The intimate nickname, said in his sexy deep timbre, liquefies my insides, but I force myself to remain strong. "Despite what you think, I actually do respect this tradition." My voice shakes as his fingers trail down my throat, discover the buttons on my dress and pluck the first three open. "Sebastian..."

"Hmm." He inhales against my hair as he cups my bra, his thumb sliding it aside to tease my nipple.

"This isn't fair."

Rolling the sensitive bud between his fingers, he kisses my temple. "All playing fair got me was: a foul mood, a raging hard-on and a dull ache in my gut that hasn't gone away since last night. I don't plan to repeat that for two more nights."

"You're going to have to," I say, trying, but failing to remain unaffected. I've never throbbed so much. The man's nearness and sexy smell alone is enough to put me in pre-orgasmic anticipation.

His hand stills, fingers pressing harder on my nipple. "Tell me you don't miss me sliding inside you."

I swallow and gasp at the sharp pleasure/pain. Even though I can't see his face, I know his blue eyes are glittering with brutal sexual intent. The man knows exactly what he's doing to my body. I twist my fingers around my purse's leather strap to keep from touching him. "I—I can wait a couple of nights."

"Liar." He bites my earlobe, his hand brushing my

purse aside to slide along my thigh, lifting the hem of my skirt. Before I can stop him, his fingers press against my underwear. "I fucking knew it. You're soaked."

I grab his wrist just as he touches the edge of my underwear, my tone desperate. "There's a bet."

"What bet?" he says, sounding suspicious.

"Cass bet me that I can't abstain from having sex with you before the wedding. I told her I plan to remain traditional. If I win, she has to take care of selling all the furniture in this apartment and negotiate with the landlord to get out of the lease. If I lose, I have to do it."

"I'll pay the damn balance of the lease," he says in a curt tone.

"If I lose, then you'll barely see me until all the furniture is gone, the place is spotless, and yes, the lease is taken care of. That could take a lot longer than a couple of days, Sebastian."

Rumbling his displeasure, he moves his mouth close to my ear. "Then you'd better be very quiet when you come, sweetheart," right as he slides a finger deep inside me.

To say my toes literally curl inside my heels when he adds a second finger is an understatement. My head falls back against the wood and I have to clamp my lips together to keep from moaning my pleasure.

"See what you're missing, gorgeous?" he says, pressing his lips against my jaw.

I can hear his smug confidence as he moves his fingers

with arousing erotic intent. With each stroke, he goes deeper until he hits my g-spot and my knees start to wobble. In less than thirty seconds he has me in a panting, hip-moving frenzy. If I don't counterstrike soon, in another minute, I'll be begging him to take me against the door.

Releasing his wrist, I quickly clasp his rock hard erection through his dress pants. "Turn about is fair play."

"That's a hell of a grip," he grunts, pulling his hand from my body to cover my hand with his.

Now that my brain can reengage, I let him go, only to trace two fingers from the base of his cock all the way to the tip. "Just checking your temperature."

"Definitely boiling point."

I love that his wit never diminishes even in moments like this. The hoarseness in his voice makes me bolder and I set my big purse on the floor, then face him and tug on his dress pants' zipper, freeing his cock from his silk boxers. I clasp his warm erection fully, and a part of me wishes I could see his expression, but then another part loves that we're exploring with only knowing touch to guide us. There's something sensually intimate about knowing your partner's body so well.

Sebastian slides his hand into my hair and yanks me against him. Groaning his pleasure against my lips, he thrusts his tongue deep, his hips pressing me against the door.

I bite his bottom lip, then accept the arousing twining

of his tongue with mine. I'll never get enough of his dominant intensity, not ever. It's one of the things I love most about my husband.

"If you don't stop kissing me, I can't use my mouth on other parts of your body," I say once he gives me a chance to breathe.

Strong hands clasp my jaw, his breath sawing. "Are you sure?"

"Can you stay quiet?"

"Can I make you scream?"

The sheer arrogance in his comment makes it hard not to smile. I love a challenge. "If you make even one sound, I'll have to stop."

His hands tighten on me, his tone gravel-rough. "Once you start, you'd better not fucking stop, Little Red."

"Then you'd better remain silent, Mister Black." I press a quick kiss to his jaw before I lower to my knees on the thick bath rug.

The moment my lips surround the tip of his cock, Sebastian's fingers slide into my hair, his hands cradling my head. I smile at the sudden intake of his breath and deep exhale out of his nose, then let him move my mouth along his silky erection several times, setting the building pace.

When the tension in his hold tells me that he's holding back his moans of pleasure, the devilish side of me decides to kick it up a notch. As he pulls his hips back, sliding me fully along his shaft, I suck and coil my tongue around him all the way to the tip.

"Goddamnit woman!" he rasps quietly, his hands fisting tight in my hair. When he grows impossibly hard and his knees bend slightly, I squeeze his muscular thighs and then move up and down his length twice more, before taking him fully down my throat.

A low, fierce rumble rushes past his lips as he goes over the edge.

When he's fully spent, Sebastian clasps my hand and quickly pulls me to my feet, his tone less tense, but somehow more lethal. "Learning just how creative you can be when I'm not allowed to fuck you senseless for two more days doesn't sit well with me."

"I've got to save *some* surprises for the wedding day." I shrug, smirking. "And you're welcome."

My husband clasps my face, big hands spreading along my jawline. Tilting my chin up, his warm lips hover close to mine. "Be glad we're already married or I'd kidnap you and make you marry me today." He kisses my lips, then my forehead before tugging me into his warm embrace, exhaling in a low voice, "I fucking love every part of you: body, mind and soul, Mrs. Blake."

I wrap my arms around his waist and bask in the sensation of his strong arms around me. "I love you too. And now that you're a bit less um…tense, I want to tell you about the article I worked on that should be releasing soon."

Just when I finish revealing who I interviewed for my article, the sound of the apartment door closing and a key turning in the lock only highlights the tense silence hanging between us.

The bathroom light suddenly snaps on. Releasing the switch, my husband zips his pants up while scowling at me from his towering height. "What the *hell*, Talia."

"I had no idea about your connection to Banks," I say, holding my hands up. "Not until I got there. I promise that I wasn't digging into your background."

"I don't give a shit about that—" He cuts himself off, his displeasure evident. "First, that neighborhood is not safe for you to be in—"

"Hence Den," I remind him, but he just talks over me, going full steam ahead.

"Second, Banks and I not only have past history, but we have some recent history as well. Stay away from him."

"And whose fault is it that I didn't know any of this?" I ask, putting my hands on my hips.

"It was related to my mom's case." Grunting, he runs a hand through his thick, black hair, leaving the short strands looking disheveled but even sexier. "As far as I'm concerned it's over."

"Ah, at least now I know why he was curious to know which Blake I'm married to."

"You told him?" His blue eyes hold mine until I nod, then they narrow to determined slits. "Pack what little you've brought here. You're coming home."

"Whoa, hold on. Is Banks truly a danger? He didn't come across as threatening. He was just forthright and curious."

"He's not a threat per se," he begins, lowering his arms.

"Then no, I won't be going home with you." When I grab my purse and open the bathroom door, my husband stalks after me into the living room.

"This isn't up for discussion, Talia."

"You're right, it's not." I open the apartment door and wait until he joins me in the hall so I can lock the door. "I love that you're protective, Sebastian, but this time it's unwarranted. I have to meet Cass for drinks in ten minutes. I suggest you go home and catch up on your sleep. Now that you *can*."

Sebastian opens his mouth to say something, then closes it. He stays broodingly silent while he follows me to my car. Once I'm seated in the driver's seat, he holds the door as I start the engine. "This discussion isn't over."

I sigh. "Send Theo if you wish. I'll be at Fine Tapas for an hour, then I'll be coming back here to sleep." Before he can say anything else, I close the door and drive off.

"Can you believe him?" I grumble at Cass as I set the small tracking device on the table.

"Where'd you find it?" she asks, picking it up to look at it.

I sigh. "I found it in my wheel well after my husband showed up at the apartment." When her eyebrow hikes, I smirk. "He promised never to put a tracker on my phone, so how else would he know how to find me?" Knowing my husband's penchant for redundancy, I checked the other wheel wells too, and sure enough I found a similar looking device in the back right one. Sneaky man thought he could hide it from me. I tossed the second one in the gurgling water fountain as I walked through the restaurant's back patio on my way inside.

"Why didn't he have his guy hack your GPS?" Cass asks as she sets the device back on the table.

"Whose side are you on?" I mutter, shaking my head. "He knows that I know how to turn it off, but at least I know how he found me at the apartment."

Cass's eyes widen. "I was *just* there."

"Oh, I know." Once I finish relaying what just happened in the bathroom, she sets her gin and tonic down, then flips her long dark hair over her shoulder and gives me the side-eye. "Wait...so you're just expecting me to skip over the part where you went down on your man, completely breaking your deal that you wouldn't have sex with him until the wedding, and go straight to the girl sympathy part?"

"Yep, it's been a hell of a day." I lift my glass of sparkling water and take a sip. "And for the record, no sex occurred, certainly not on *my* part."

Cass purses her lips doubtfully, then nods toward my glass. "You sure you don't want something stronger?"

"No, Sebastian has me too wound up. If I drink anything, the sugar will make me toss and turn all night. I didn't sleep well last night and need to catch up."

"You can always have one of these," she suggests, lifting her cocktail.

"You know I hate gin," I say, wrinkling my nose. Sighing, I lift my shoulders and let them fall. "Please tell me everything's going to run like clockwork for tomorrow's rehearsal. I need to hear some good news right now."

Cass pulls a folder and pen out of her big purse and quickly flips it open on the table. "Mina and I have our dresses—seriously, thank you for choosing classic black—and of course the Blake men already own their tuxes. The flowers are ordered, your favorite caterer is confirmed with all the foods you requested. Delivery times and locations are confirmed with each of the vendors."

I smile as she meticulously checks off the list while talking. "Thank you for saving me, Cass. This will be like riding a bike by the time your wedding rolls around."

"My pleasure. You know I love creating fairytales. Though it's so much more fun when it's real life instead of in photos." She grins, then continues down the list. "I've coordinated with the church about the rehearsal. Pastor Meyer expects you, Sebastian and the rest of the wedding party to be at the church at four-thirty tomorrow." Pausing, she glances up from the paper, dark eyebrows raised over light brown eyes. "By the way, the pastor's only letting you two slide from counseling because of his longstanding relationship with the Blake family."

"So it has nothing to do with the fact we're already married?"

She snickers at my sarcasm, then returns to her list. "The RSVPs are flooding in. Though, I'm surprised I haven't seen one from your aunt."

The knowledge the invitation is still sitting in my purse burns through my mind, but Cass knows nothing about my aunt's past actions, so I just wave and mutter, "Don't worry about it."

"If you say so," she says, then lifts her eyebrows. "Speaking of family…when I pressed Mina, she confessed that her mother was the one who asked her for a photo to put the engagement announcement in the paper at Adam Blake's insistence."

My immediate irritation that Sebastian's nasty stepmother, Isabel, was the one who submitted the announcement to the paper completely slips away. The fact she did it for Sebastian's father means that Adam is trying to rectify all the years he didn't acknowledge his illegitimate son by making a big deal over a Blake's upcoming wedding. That makes my heart melt.

Cass pauses when her phone beeps with a text. She smiles and taps out a response, then sets her phone down and starts to go over the itinerary once more.

I raise my eyebrow. "Who was that?"

"Oh, that was Mina asking if I was truly taking care of your entire schedule for the wedding so you had nothing to worry about."

I lift my glass to her in salute. "Did you tell her that you are?"

As Cass nods, I get a text from Mina.

I just checked with Cass to make sure you're not overloaded with wedding stuff. Thank you so much for watching Josi tonight, Talia. You have no idea how relieved I am. It'll be my first time leaving her and who better than with her godparents. Can you believe it...this will be my first night out since she was born! On a date, no less. I'm so excited! Thank you again! I told Sebastian I'll pick her up around eleven.

Tapping out a "you're welcome and have a good time" text to Mina, I mutter, "He has no shame" as I put my phone in my purse and lay a few dollars on the table.

"Wait? Where are you going?"

"My *husband* just found a way to force me to come home."

"Really?" She laughs, intrigued. "How?"

"Godparent duty. Any other time I would look forward to babysitting little Josi for an evening, but the timing of this visit has Sebastian's fingerprints all over it."

"You've got to give the man props for being inventive," she says, eyes dancing with amusement.

"I don't *have* to give him anything. And get that smug look off your face. You're NOT winning this bet."

Her eyebrows shoot up innocently. "I didn't say anything."

"The only thing missing is you rubbing your hands together in glee.

Snickering, Cass lifts a pinky finger to the corner of her pursed lips in a Dr. Evil impression.

"*Ugh*. I'm out of here. Night, Cass."

"Don't forget...tomorrow at four-thirty at the church for rehearsal!" Cass calls after me.

I turn and blow her a kiss before I walk out the door.

CHAPTER FOUR

Talia

Sebastian is sitting on the couch with Josi tucked against him when I step off the elevator into our penthouse apartment. The adorable sight knocks some of the frustrated wind out of me.

"Look who it is, Josi-bean!" He lifts the TV remote and lowers the sound on the sports recaps. "Aunt Talia's home."

Josi's curly blonde ringlets bounce as she swivels her head in my direction. She instantly smiles around her bottle and waves her arms but doesn't stop sucking.

When I move to sit down on the sofa and hold my finger out for her to clasp onto it, he says lightly, "What are you doing here? I thought you were having drinks with Cass?"

I rub my thumb over Josi's tiny fingers curled around mine. "I can't believe you used godparent babysitting duty to get me to come home," I say in a light tone to keep Josi from sensing that I'm not super happy with him.

"You didn't need to come home, Talia. We've already had dinner and are just chilling with an after dinner cordial." Sebastian pauses and lifts the bottle up to see if his niece is done. Josi begins to wail and he immediately plops it right back into her mouth, murmuring, "Sorry, Bean. You stopped sucking. Yeah, I know your aunt can be very distracting." When she smiles at his deep voice and makes contented gurgling sounds around her bottle, he flicks his gaze to me. "Josi and I have got it covered."

She's still clutching my finger tight as she begins to lightly pat her uncle's big hand holding her bottle. Of course now I feel foolish for assuming he orchestrated this entire evening with an agenda in mind. Apparently, he's better at this babysitting thing than I realized. Watching Sebastian and his niece together makes me feel like an intruder horning in on their blissful evening. Still, that tracking device is burning a hole in the bottom of my purse. When did he put it on my car?

Just as I smile down at Josi's adorable face, he says, "Am I supposed to give her a bath? While we're in there, I think I'm going to work on this potty training thing. Diapers are a pain. I'll bet I can teach her to use the potty in a day."

I snap my gaze to his in an "are you kidding me?" look. *Uh yeah, I don't buy that innocent act for a minute.* He definitely engineered this. Just like he's going to pretend he didn't put a tracking device on my car. "You can't give her a bath. We don't have any baby soap or shampoo. I'm sure your sister will give her one in the morning." I pull the diaper bag on the floor next to the sofa over and retrieve a diaper, the wipes, and the changing pad. "And you are not going to freak this child out by hovering her little butt over the toilet and commanding that she go potty."

He frowns at me. "Of course I won't hover her over the toilet. She can sit up on her own now. I'll just set her on the seat."

I arch an eyebrow. "She'll fall in. Baby's need a baby potty to learn to use the bathroom, which doesn't happen until they're at least eight months older than she is right now, by the way." I lift the diaper stuff I pulled out. "Do this once she finishes that bottle."

"Don't diapers last all day? They need to make diapers like camel humps."

Men. "She needs a change now," I say, shaking my head.

"How can you tell—" A pause, then his nose wrinkles. "Never mind."

Silently dying of laughter, I walk over to the bookshelves to retrieve a couple of books I bought for when Josi did come to visit.

"I set the portable crib up in the guest bedroom. Mina says Josi usually goes to bed around eight." He pauses to look down at Josi and she stares up at him with adoring eyes. "Though she doesn't look sleepy to me."

"You should keep her on her routine as much as possible," I suggest, handing him the books. "These should help."

"Where are you going?" he calls after me once I start toward our bedroom.

"I'm changing clothes."

"But—" He holds the diaper up, a hopeful look on his face.

"You said you've got it covered," I say, before entering our bedroom.

Sebastian doesn't know that I stayed just inside the doorway, listening to him. I have to cover my mouth to keep from snickering when he says, "Did you see how deftly your aunt avoided doody duty?" The rip of her diaper precedes Josi's giggles of delight. "All right, all right. Quit squirming or I'll have to call you Jumping Bean from now on." Josi giggles again and a few seconds pass. "There, now you're ready for the next explosion. How about we go get our jammies on? I think your mom set them on the guest bed…"

As his voice fades into the guest bedroom, my amusement turns into surprised appreciation and my heart swells. For all his tough guy exterior, I had no idea how patient my SEAL-trained husband could be with kids. What if I'm a terrible mother and freak out with a new baby? Thoughts about my mom's indifference after I was born, and then her suicide, creep into my mind, spreading like a disease. Sebastian said he wants a family one day, but watching over a toddler like I did with Amelia is nothing compared to the exhausting, never-ending vigilance of taking care of a newborn.

Mina said Sebastian really helped her when she first got home from the hospital as a single mother. At the time, I assumed she meant for moral support, but after watching how comfortable he is with Josi, he truly was the best big brother ever to her. I consider myself beyond lucky to have married someone who's not afraid of raising kids, while at the same time his easy confidence makes me question if I'll ever be as naturally relaxed as he seems to be.

Sighing over my unease, I kick off my heels, then slip out of my dress. I start to open my dresser drawer and my gaze snags on the picture that I had drawn for Amelia of our names inside two hearts. Even though the same "Two Lias" picture, along with a photo of our goddaughter is inside the locket I'm wearing, Sebastian also had the artwork printed and framed for our bedroom. I kiss two fingers and press them to the glass, my heart twisting for her loss. "He would've charmed you too, sweet Amelia."

I couldn't prevent her tragic death, but I was a good big sister. The fact we weren't blood related never mattered.

The memory of her little body squirming close in a hug might be bittersweet, but it helps ease my worry a little as I pull out my favorite pajama set. Once I'm dressed, hopefully I'll get a chance to cuddle with Josi before she falls asleep.

Sebastian's deep voice floats from the guest bedroom as he reads "Guess How Much I Love You" to his niece. He's leaning against the headboard, Josi tucked into the crook of his arm. It's such a sweet moment, I turn and retrieve my purse. Setting it on the island, I quickly dig through it, pulling things out of the way to retrieve my phone, then quietly grab a shot and send his sister a text with the image.

Uncle Seb has her completely enthralled!

Mina's quick *Awwww, he's the best* reply pings on my phone, drawing Sebastian's attention.

"Aunt Talia's come to read too. Then it's off to sleep for you."

When he tickles her belly, Josi's peals of laughter make me smile. I step into the room and pull her blanket from inside the crib, then lift the other book from the end of the bed and lean against the headboard bedside my husband. "Are you ready for *Goodnight Moon?*

Josi's eyes widen and she smacks her hands together. "Oon, Ahhya."

Sebastian glances my way, then back to Josi. "Did you just say Talia?"

Crawling into my lap, Josi grabs her blanket in a tight hold, then settles her back against my chest and smacks at the book in my hand. "Oon! Oon, Ahhya!"

When I don't start reading right away, she puckers her little lips and looks right at her uncle. "Bye-bye."

I can't help but burst out laughing when Sebastian shakes his head and says, "Guess I've been dismissed." Leaning over, he kisses Josi on top of her head, then slides off the bed. "Night, Josi-bean."

The moment he pulls the door partway closed behind him, Josi turns her big light green eyes up to me and pats my cheek. "Oon."

I kiss the inside of her hand and snuggle her tiny body close. Pushing my nose into her soft curls, I inhale her baby powder smell before reading the opening lines of the book.

Josi asks me to read *Goodnight Moon* again as soon as I'm done. The little tyke finally dozes off right at the very end of the second round. Lifting her, I lay her down in her crib and smile that even in sleep, she never lets go of the blanket.

Turning down the nightstand lamp all the way to dim, I walk over to the door and lean around it, watching her as I begin to pull it closed. I freeze when the hinge creaks and Josi stirs and whimpers. After a couple of sighs, she falls back to sleep. I exhale and pull the door the rest of the way until it's shut.

The living room lights are out and Sebastian has changed into lounge pants and a dark t-shirt. He's standing next to the wall of windows, his wrists folded at his back. New York's cityscape creates an impressive backdrop in the distance. He'd poured me a glass of red wine and set it on the table near the windows. *What is he thinking about?*

"The view is always impressive," I say as I move to stand beside him.

He glances my way, his gaze sweeping over me. "I absolutely agree."

My face heats when I realize he's referring to me, but just when I turn to say something, he shifts his attention back to the city. "As payback for something I did that pissed him off when I was young, Banks told Hayes where to find me. And because Banks led Hayes straight to me, that's the night I lost my mother."

"I'm so...sorry, Sebastian." My stomach pitches and I know my face must suddenly be very pale. "I wish you had told me. I had no idea."

"I honestly never thought the two worlds would collide."

Glancing my way, he slides his hand under my hair and cups my neck, running his thumb down the side of my throat. "Once I learned of Bank's part in my mother's death, I called a police buddy of mine and told him where to find an entire warehouse of goods. Banks had been stashing stuff there since I was a teen. I knew they couldn't tie it to him, because he was always a careful bastard, but the loss would leave a dent. As far as I was concerned, we were even."

"Except you didn't expect me to interview him."

He frowns, his thumb pausing on my skin. "Now that he knows I have someone I care about, that's dangerous leverage."

I lift my eyebrows. "Today's engagement announcement would've clued him into that anyway."

His fingers tighten slightly on my neck. "I haven't had a chance to rip into Isabel for that yet."

"My understanding is that your father requested the announcement be sent out." I try to gauge his thoughts, wondering what he's thinking. "Adam is trying, Sebastian. Let your father be proud of his son."

When he just grunts in response, I circle back to his concern about the interview. "Banks honestly didn't seem angry or vengeful when he mentioned you. Annoyed yes. He even said we're alike…" I pause and smirk. "But I believe it'll be okay."

"I hope you're right and I'm just being overprotective."

"You are." Turning, I lift the glass of wine from the table. "You should drink this tonight. You never relax… and well, you should."

"Only if you sit with me," he says, taking the glass from me. I nod and he gestures to the table. "Have a seat."

Happy he's willing, I perch on the edge of the table and

lean back on my hands, slowly kicking my feet back and forth. "Take a sip and try to pick out the peppery notes and other flavors. Enjoy the experience. Show me that you know how to relax."

"There's only one thing that relaxes me." Giving me a pointed look, he takes a sip of the wine.

"You've already had your *relaxation* for the day. Now try the liquid version."

"I will."

When he sets the glass on the table between my legs, then grips my thighs in a firm hold, my heart rate jumps. "What are you doing?"

"The wine lacks a key ingredient."

"What's that?" I ask, my breath catching at the heated way he's staring at my mouth.

"Talia notes are missing from this liquid relaxation experience."

My stomach tightens and desire floods my core. Every part of me tingles when he pushes my thighs apart and steps between them. "*That* isn't on the wine's list of ingredients, Mister Black." I quickly put my hands over his before he can touch places that'll send my heart soaring. If I let this continue, I'll be begging him to take me to bed.

"Do you want me to drink the wine?"

I hold his steady gaze. This isn't about the wine. It's about my husband trusting in life's journey and allowing himself to just *be* without feeling the need to be constantly on guard. I know being reminded of his mother's death has a lot to do with his tension, but it must be exhausting walking around like that all the time. "I want you to be able to enjoy a glass of wine every so often, Sebastian."

"Then the only way that's happening…" His voice drops to a deeper timbre as he moves the glass of wine to my right on the table. "Is if I have it *with* you. Now lift that sweet ass, Little Red."

Desire burns in his eyes as I bite my lip. The moment I lift my hips, he instantly slides my silk pajama pants and underwear off, dropping them onto the floor.

The table is cool and my skin prickles, a shiver rushing through me.

"Cold?"

Boldness thrums through my veins, warming my blood and I shake my head. "Just wondering if the marriage of the two will meet your palate's approval."

His eyebrow hikes and lust flashes in his gaze. "I'm certain this blend will only grow better with age." Warm hands cover my thighs, gliding along them. "Slide back a little."

Curious what he's up to, I do as he commands, keeping my attention focused on his hands.

When my husband pulls two long swaths of red silk from his pants' pockets, my gaze jerks to my purse on the island. "Did you take my—Sebastian, that was for something else."

"I'm sure whatever it was...you'll feel this was more than worth it, Little Red," he says with toe-curling confidence as he expertly ties the two ends of the four-inch wide strips together into a bow. With a dark, sexy smile, he lays the bow against my belly, then leans close to cross the trailing ends behind my back and then back around the front of my body. "Bend your knees, beautiful."

The huskiness in his voice intrigues me. "No hands this time?" I tease as he loops the silky material from the outside of my thighs around to the insides.

He glances up after doing the same to my knees, a smirk on his face. "I have a feeling you'll want to hold onto something more substantial, like the table."

"Good to know," I say lightheartedly to cover my nervousness as he drops the trailing ends of the sashes down either side of the table. "Are you done decorating the bottle?"

He releases a low chuckle as he bends over to tuck the sashes' ends under the table, pulling them to the table's end. When he lifts one sash up, then begins to loop it around my ankle, his focus methodical and intense, my lighthearted amusement shifts to nervous anticipation. Sebastian never does anything without purpose. What is his goal tonight?

He holds my gaze as he wraps the end around the table leg, then gives the material a firm tug. The wrapped silk zips over my skin in a quick burn, the instant tightening forcing my knee outward while also anchoring my foot to the table's corner. "This is not a bottle decoration," he rumbles after he secures the end around my ankle, then wraps my other leg in the same fashion.

Pressing a kiss on a spot where the silk isn't covering my skin on my inner thigh, he glances up at me and clasps my thighs in a possessive hold. The silk under my hips gives him a slick surface to play with and with a quick jerk he pulls me closer. I gasp as the wrapped material pulls my knees impossibly wide, while the silky pulley system he's created clasps my ankles in a firm lover's hold.

"No, sweet Talia..." he continues as he lifts the glass of wine in salute. "You're the main course. The wine will only be used to complement your delicious flavor."

Leaning forward, he runs the cool stem along my inner thigh, then slides it in between my lower lips, pressing it against my clit. "Unbutton your top."

I feel exposed and vulnerable already. My shirt is my last line of defense against his penetrating gaze. "Do you really need—"

"Do you want to be able to button it back?"

His tone is clipped, arrogant. Dominant. He won't think twice about shredding it. My hands shake a little as I unbutton the top and let it fall open. Cool air hits my exposed breasts, making the peaks harden and stand up at attention. Sebastian sets the glass down and dips two fingers into the dark liquid, then traces them across my nipples and down to my navel.

My belly tenses with his touch and my heart thumps at a rapid pace as he slowly pulls me even closer and leans to hover his lips over my nipple. Warm breath bathes my breast before he runs his tongue slowly over my prickled skin.

Loving the intimacy, I slide my hands into his hair and try to tug him close, but my husband won't let me change his pace. He sucks my nipple into his mouth and just when I think he's going to tug hard and make me shiver more, he shifts to the other breast and starts the same torturous process all over again. "This is my idea of a full-bodied wine," he rumbles appreciatively against my body as he clasps my waist in a firm hold and runs his tongue slowly down to my bellybutton.

I begin to pant when he rubs his nose in the tiny triangle of hair between my legs, then moan as he clasps my ass and bites down on the left side of my mons and then the right. Each nip dominant and aggressive. "I love that this pussy is all mine to completely possess."

He glances up at me, flashing a smile of sheer arrogance. "And I do plan to reacquaint myself with every lovely bit of it until you're writhing with the need to come."

The look of determination on his face worries me. Does that mean he's not going to finish? Will he leave me hanging until I'm a blubbering mess? I'm throbbing already and the way he's gripping me doesn't bode well for me being able to walk myself to the bedroom later. Sebastian carrying me will not be a good scenario for abstaining. If that man gets me anywhere near a bed, it'll be my undoing.

I fist my hand in his hair. "If you leave me hanging so help me, Sebastia—"

I cut myself off when he thrusts his tongue deep into my channel. Pressing a chaste kiss there, he smiles. "I love the way you taste too much to do that, Little Red. If anything...you're going to lose count of the number of orgasms you have tonight."

Sitting up, he lifts the glass and just when I think he's going to take another sip, he tilts it and dribbles the dark liquid from my bellybutton to my mons. It's cold and erotic and I bite my lip to hold back the shocking gasp. Shivering in anxious anticipation, I force my hands that intuitively want to wipe the wine off me to stay relaxed by my sides on the table. Setting the glass down, my husband's gaze holds mine with the look of a starving man as he flattens his hands on the table, caging me in.

"You might want to hold on, Little Red. I promise this is one wine tasting you're never going to forget. There is, of course...only one rule."

"What's that?" I whisper, so ready to feel his mouth on my body once more.

"Don't spill the wine."

I stare down at the liquid pooling in my navel and quivering on my lower belly. "What happens if it spills?"

Sebastian gives me a wolfish smile. "I get to take you to bed."

Oh God, the man always makes me squirm. I can't do this. No, I *have* to do this. I narrow my gaze, then tilt my chin, accepting his challenge. Slowly lifting my arms above my head, I grab onto the table's edge and slightly arch my back so my boobs draw his attention too. "That red marring my skin must be driving you mad. You'd better take care of that for me, Mister Black."

But instead of going for the goods, my husband surprises the hell out of me by pressing his lips to the skin above my ankle. I wiggle my toes and try to keep my breathing even as he moves up to my calf and nips at the muscle. Then he slides to the uncovered area just above my knee. I'm quivering by the time he makes his way to the sensitive juncture where my leg meets my body.

"Taste me, Sebastian!" I demand, then growl my frustration when he leans over and sucks the wine from my navel. "That's not what I meant."

He ignores my grumble and bites down on the inside of my other thigh. I jump, then shift my hip to keep the red liquid from rolling off my belly. "Inflicting pain isn't playing fair, husband!"

He jerks his gaze up from kissing the same spot. "Leaving my bed isn't fair either, *wife*."

"You got your dessert," I say, my breathing shallow.

Sebastian slides his hands under my thighs, gripping

them in a firm hold. "Desserts never provide the necessary nutrients a full course can. I'm a steak, potatoes, salad and bread kind of guy."

"Are you comparing me to your favorite meal?" I ask, mock-offended.

Sebastian runs his tongue along my sensitive folds and groans his approval. "Damn straight. You're definitely my favorite *hot* meal," he says as he devours my body with such brutal intensity that I barely keep myself from arching off the table as my vision begins to blur.

Thoughts of wine spilling, weddings, and friend's bets evaporate from my mind. My husband plays my body like the seasoned dominant he is. He takes me to the brink, then pulls me back over and over, leaving me delirious with the need to climax and beyond frustrated with the desire to move.

"Please, Sebastian, just let me come. I'll do whatever you want. Stop torturing me."

"I never want to wake up without you again."

I close my eyes, so filled with building tension I can no longer feel my hands holding onto the table. "Fine," I hiss, my sex throbbing from being denied release.

As he slides two fingers deep inside my core, I moan and tears spill with the slight rush of relief.

"That's not an answer, sweetheart. I want to hear you *say* it."

Sebastian's expression is ruthless, his touch purposeful

as he turns his fingers and hits my G-spot with slow, deliberate strokes.

My whole body jerks to my rising heart rate and my thighs quiver. I can't edge away. Instead, the tug of the silk forcing me to stay open to his every whim only adds to the maddening eroticism. "You'll never have to wake up without me again. God, Sebastian...just give me release!"

A moment suspends between us, his gaze locking with mine. Hooking his fingers inside me, Sebastian lets out a feral grunt and yanks me forward, the glide of silk enhancing his primal move. Lapping up the last of the wine, he latches onto my clit with unparalleled fierceness and I arch, my vision blurring. I bite back the wail of animalistic approval that shoots to my throat and release my hold on the table to jam my aching fingers into his hair.

Tugging hard, I press against him, my heart racing too fast for my chest to contain it. Once my climax rolls over my body in shuddering waves of pure bliss, Sebastian doesn't relent. One orgasm after another tears through me. After the fourth one hits, then starts to build into another, I tear at his hair until he grunts in pain. "No more, Sebastian," I pant. "I can't...too much..."

Straightening, my husband tugs at the bow on my waist while he downs the last of the wine. Once the ribbon unravels, he does the same to the bows at my ankles before lifting me as if I weigh nothing. "Never leave me again," he says roughly, running his nose along my temple. "No matter where you lay your head, Little Red, mine will always be next to yours."

My arms and legs feel like jelly. I'm breathing too hard to comment, my heart still pounding from Sebastian's orgasm bullet train. All I can do is bob my head against his chest as he carries me to our bedroom.

Our room is comforting in its quiet stillness as he lays me in our bed. The pillows and smooth sheets smell of Sebastian's appealing masculine scent. I take advantage of the darkness to lean into the pillow and inhale deeply as he strips out of his clothes. I can no more resist him pulling me into the circle of his arms than breathe. And at this moment, I don't want to.

He kisses my forehead, his voice a low, promising rumble. "Close your eyes for a few, Talia. I'm nowhere near done."

"Be sure to go check on Josi," I say sleepily. His sister won't be here for three hours. With a promise like that, I should be anxious that he'll have more time to work his magic on me, but my brain is still in fog mode. Rubbing my nose against his warm chest, I close my eyes and drift into an exhausted sleep.

Sebastian getting out of bed wakes me. I groggily follow and slip on a silk robe while he steps into lounge pants and a t-shirt.

I have just enough time to stuff my PJs and the red silk sashes into my purse before Mina steps off the elevator.

Sebastian greets his little sister, arms crossed.

"He'd better have been a gentleman."

Mina rolls her eyes. "He was fine, Seb. More a friend than true date material. It was just nice to get out for a little while." She includes me in the conversation as I approach. "Did Josi give you any trouble?"

"No. She was an angel," I say smiling.

"After she kicked her uncle out so Talia could read to her."

Mina snickers at Sebastian's disgruntled tone. "My daughter definitely has a mind of her own. I'll just grab her so you two can go back to bed. Why you're both working tomorrow I have no idea," she says, shaking her head. "I took a week off before my wedding."

As she starts to walk away, Sebastian's tone turns serious. "Speaking of our wedding, please don't give any more pictures to Isabel."

"I know my mom's not your favorite person." Mina turns to face us once more. "But she just wanted to please our father."

"There's a reason you and Calder are the only ones in our family who know about this place. My privacy is important to me. That extends to personal photos."

"Maybe if you tried more..." Mina starts to say, but seeing her brother's closed expression, she sighs and pushes her long blonde hair over her shoulder. "Okay, I get it, Seb."

As she walks into the guest bedroom to pick up her sleeping daughter, I whisper to Sebastian, "Are you ever going to tell her just how devious her mother can be? I'm a little concerned about Isabel's influence over Josi."

"You don't have to worry. Isabel is too self-centered to spend more than a few minutes with her granddaughter, let alone babysit. She'll expect Josi to always be dressed appropriately in public and to not act out, but that's about it. My sister knows Isabel's less-than-stellar tendencies, but I refuse to destroy Mina's illusion that her mother is basically a good person beneath all that superficiality. It would crush her."

I watch his half-sister cooing to her sleepy baby who's fussing from being roused. "Mina's stronger than you think."

"Maybe," he says, looking contemplative. "But my father would never forgive himself if he ever found out Isabel paid someone to take me out once she learned of my existence."

I lift my eyebrows, surprised to hear him protecting Adam's feelings. "Are you starting to *like* your father, Sebastian?"

"Let's not get carried away. I always put family first." Hooking his arm around my shoulder, he pulls me close and presses his lips to my temple, then husks in my ear, "Go warm the bed for me, sexy. I'll lock up."

I grab my purse off the table and head back to our

room, so nervous my hands are shaking. *How will I keep that man at bay for one more day?*

When I glance down at my purse, I exhale my nervous tension as an idea forms.

CHAPTER FIVE

Sebastian

After my sister leaves, I make sure the elevator is locked, then turn off the lights. My heart thumps and my dick turns rock-hard as I head for my bedroom. I can already taste Talia's sweetness on my tongue. I'm so fucking ready to slide inside her warmth my balls are aching. I halt in the doorway at the sight of the tracking device from Talia's car on my pillow.

Well fuck.

She's leaning on her elbow, her silk nightshirt fully buttoned. "I'm assuming this happened because you were so worried about me?"

Her tone is even, which means she's not really angry, but I answer honestly as I approach the bed. "You dismissed your detail. I needed peace of mind."

"Theo's not my babysitter." My wife gestures to the device. "Tomorrow we'll get back to clearer thinking."

"My thinking is sharp at all times."

"Even in redundancy mode," she says, an edge of sarcasm lacing her tone.

I shrug out of my shirt and pick up the tracker, my gaze heavy on hers. "Your safety will always come first, Talia. That's a promise I made you before we got married."

She sighs and tucks a lock of her auburn hair behind her ear. "I've been taking care of myself most of my life, Sebastian. You need to have a little faith."

"It's not *you* I worry about," I say, scowling. "It's all the asshole schmucks out there."

We stare at each other in silence and when I see her gaze stray to my naked chest, my dick instantly stirs back to full attention. I move to pull the covers back, but she shakes her head.

"What happened to 'my head always rests where yours does'?"

Sitting up, she grabs the cover lying across the bottom of our bed and spreads it out beside her. "Your head *will* be right beside mine," she says as she pats the blanket beside her.

My gaze narrows. "You're serious?"

"I'm serious about two things: I would like you to trust that I'll do what it takes to protect myself. And yes, I'm sincere about abstaining until we walk down the aisle."

Grumbling, I set the tracking device down on the nightstand, turn out the light and climb into bed, pulling the thin cover over me. She tenses slightly when I wrap my arm around her waist and tug her back against me despite the covers between us. "Don't think for one minute I'm not going to hold you close, sweetheart."

"You're incorrigible," she sighs in the darkness.

"Determined," I whisper against her ear, then plant a warm kiss on the back of her neck. "But since we're laying here awake, why don't you tell me about my ring."

"Never!" Talia laughs softly. "And no more turning this apartment inside-out looking for it, because I'm not telling you anything about it, other than to say it's *not* here, Mr. Sneaky Pants. Who knew the man I married hated surprises? I'm just glad I have a heads up about this tendency of yours before your birthday rolls around."

I shrug. "I like knowing what's coming. What metal is it?"

"Not telling."

"Is it yellow? White? Black?"

"Nice try."

"Stones?" I grumble, not liking the idea of any kind of gemstone in my ring.

"It's mini handcuffs," she says on a snicker.

Snorting, I kiss the back of her head. "Close your eyes, sexy. One more night of torture until I get to make you mine all over again."

"That didn't sound at *all* territorial," she says through a yawn as she slides our fingers together.

"Damn straight, Little Red," I rumble, tucking our folded hands between her breasts.

The sound of her low laugh makes me smile in the darkness.

"I love you too, Mister Black."

I lift the tracking device from my nightstand and lean up on my elbow to watch my wife sleeping peacefully. With the sun shining on her vibrant red hair splayed across the pillow, and one long, shapely leg thrown out of the covers as she faces me on her side, she's the picture of well-tumbled. I might be her Rainbow Master in bed, but whether she realizes it or not, she has delivered on her promise to help me see life's colors through her eyes.

I no longer resent the loss of my color vision. Yes, it's a fucking annoyance at times to be mostly limited to the gray spectrum, especially since no one at BLACK Security knows the truth, but I count myself blessed that I can at least see the brighter end of the red spectrum. Talia has no idea how much I love staring at her hair. The pleasure I derive from seeing that bit of color surrounding her face each day is indescribable. I'll never tire of it.

I curl my fingers tight around the tracker in my hand to keep from reaching over and running my fingers through the silky auburn strands. She looks so relaxed, I don't want to disturb her just yet. While she's sleeping, she's not off interviewing past enemies and stirring up old wounds. Here, in our home, I know she's safe. And that's the thing that's such a constant kick in the gut…worrying about her safety with her job. It puts her in harm's way more than it fucking should, but I would never tell her to quit.

I can't believe she's writing an article about Banks as a savior for his neighborhood. How fucking ironic is that? Talia might think he's fine with her connection to me, but my jaw still pops a little each time I move it a certain way from that sucker punch he inflicted during my last "conversation" with him about someone I care about. He might not be directly responsible for my mother's death, but he's connected. If that fucker even dares to look at Talia sideways, I'll destroy everything he has built without a second thought.

The plastic casing around the tracker in my hand suddenly cracks, yanking my attention back to the present. Exhaling, I ease my tight hold on the device.

Talia wants me to relax, but my dark past and SEAL training have conditioned me to protect. Being on alert isn't something I can just switch off. It's in my DNA. But pleasurable distractions…hell yeah…that I can get on board with. My gaze slides down to her shirt. It came unbuttoned in her sleep, exposing the peachy curve of her breast. My mouth waters at the fullness. I didn't get to spend as much time on them as I would've liked last night. Thoughts of our evening rushes forth—the memories of her body shuddering under my mouth and hands and the sweet taste of her on my tongue—and my morning wood instantly hardens to painful ball-throbbing levels.

I force my gaze to her face and memorize her long lashes shadowing her curved cheekbones and the bow of her lips. Fucking hell I want her, but since sex isn't on the agenda, an excuse to touch her while also adding to my own peace of mind will have to do.

Sitting up, I lean over and give her sweet ass a whack. "Wake up, gorgeous!"

"Ow!" she says, instantly glaring at me as she rubs her rear through the silky material of her underwear. "Do you have a death wish this morning?"

"You said last night you want me to trust that you can handle yourself. Well, there's no better time than the present. How about a morning lesson in self-defense?"

Talia scowls at me as she tosses her bedhead mane over her shoulder. "That was meant figuratively, Sebastian."

Standing, I set the tracking gadget on the nightstand and cross my arms. "You're going to 'figuratively' defend yourself in the face of an attacker?"

"Of course not. I would…"

My eyebrow hikes. "What? What would you do?" When her only answer is to glare at me, I gesture to the open space in front of our bed. "Come here. This will only take a few minutes, but it could save your life."

"I'm no SEAL," she says on a snort as she crawls out of bed and moves to stand in front of me.

"The goal here, Little Red, is to give you a chance to get away from your attacker, not beat them to a pulp. That's my job. Are you ready?"

Nodding, she puts her hands up, her fists curled tight.

She looks so adorable, with her tousled hair, shirt partially unbuttoned and no pants on that I can't help but grab her fist and press a kiss to her knuckles. "Even in this feisty pose, you're tempting as hell."

Talia quickly lands a punch to my side with her free fist. I grunt and she jumps back from my loosened hold. Bouncing on the balls of her feet like a boxer, she raises her fists, ready once more. "See…I improvised."

I step forward and immediately encircle her throat. "Things can change on a dime. Be ready." I don't squeeze, but when she intuitively reaches for my wrists and tries to push my hands off to free herself, I say in an even tone, "What you're doing will cut your breathing off. Raise your hands above your head, forming a letter A around my wrists."

When she gives me a doubtful look, I wait for her to comply. Once she sighs and does as I ask, I continue, "Now throw your arms down to one side, fast and hard."

She quickly drops her arms to the left toward the floor and my hands are immediately pulled from her throat.

"Ha, that worked well."

"You should be running away at this moment, not gloating," I lightly reprimand.

Nodding, she stands at attention and gives a quick salute. "Okay, got it. Any other tips?"

Taking her by the shoulders, I walk her into a corner of our bedroom. "The last thing you ever want is to be backed into a corner, Talia. But if you find yourself trapped, fight like mad and give it everything you've got to be free." I lift her hands up toward my face. "The eyes are as vulnerable as balls. Keep your fingers slightly bent and jab at them with just as much gusto. If you're being attacked and you can't stab your fingers into his eyes first, then knee him in the balls. The second he reaches down to defend his maimed junk, go for his eyes or chop at his exposed throat if you can't get to the eyes. Once he stumbles, get out of there." I lift her arm and bend it, tapping on her elbow. "Don't forget that your elbow is one of the strongest weapons in your arsenal; use it for a blow to the head or jam into his chest if he's behind you."

Turning her around, I hook my arm over her chest. The moment I pull her against me in a firm hold, her feminine scent hits me in the gut. "You smell so damn good," I murmur, running my nose along her throat."

"Ahem…defense lessons," she says on a soft laugh.

"Right." I smirk and tighten my hold slightly. "If your attacker is behind you and he has your arms trapped, head butt him to free yourself. Once your arms are free, turn and follow my other advice about vulnerable spots: jab, knee, and elbow, then run like hell."

Once I release her and she turns around, her eyes spark with determination. "We have five minutes before we have to get ready for work. Any other moves you'd like to show me?"

I give a wolfish smile. "I can think of plenty of moves I'd like to show you."

"Focus, husband." She grins, shaking her head.

I nod and clasp her wrist. Tugging her to her back on the carpet, I trap her hands on the floor, leaning on my knees over her. "Think you can budge me?"

She grunts as she tries to tug free of my hands. "Two-hundred-plus pounds of pure muscle is hard to move."

"My weight doesn't matter. Use my size to your advantage here. You just need to knock me off balance to be free."

When she stares up at me like I'm a puzzle she's trying to figure out, I chuckle. "I can see that brain of yours spinning. Any thoughts?"

"Just one." When she whispers the next part and I dip my head slightly to hear what she's saying, she folds her right elbow in and upward. Trapping my arm against her head at the same time she bends her right knee and hooks her foot around my calf, she lifts her hips high and jams her left hip against my body, shoving my body over with all her strength.

I end up on my back with my wife kneeling between my thighs, fingers in claw mode, ready to gouge my eyes out.

"Now you're completely at my mercy!" As she laughs and falls against me, thumping her hands triumphantly on my chest, my nightstand alarm goes off. I quickly grip her waist and pull her up my body until we're nose to nose.

I'm proud as hell that she caught on so fast, while sexual tension and annoyance at the alarm's timing buzzes through my veins. "Good strategic move, Little Red. But unless you want to be at *my* mercy, you should stop rubbing your half-naked sexiness against my neglected body parts and hit the shower."

Pressing her lips to mine, she quickly rolls off me before I can lock her to me and deepen the kiss. "Be back here at three to get ready for rehearsal," she says as she walks toward the bathroom.

"Theo's back on duty," I call after her.

She turns before she reaches the bathroom, her eyebrow arched. "So much for self-defense lessons."

I lean on my elbow, my gaze drilling into hers. "He's your shadow until the wedding is over, Talia."

After she nods her agreement and reaches for the doorjamb to turn into the bathroom, I say, "We'll reassess after that."

Talia quickly turns back, frowning. "Sebastian—"

The second alarm goes off just then from the nightstand. I point to my ear. "Can't hear you."

I hold back my chuckle when she throws her hands up. Just as she starts to shut the door, the alarm turns itself off. Talia pokes her head back out and says, "Oh, I meant to tell you…after talking to my dad, I've decided to invite my aunt to the wedding."

When she quickly shuts the door before I can voice my opinion, I scowl and call out, "Definitely reassessing, Talia!"

CHAPTER SIX

Talia

"Are you kidding me?"

"Keep your voice down," Stan says to me while Nathan quickly moves to shut our boss's office door.

"It's out of our hands, Talia." Stan closes the folder with Bank's interview in it and moves it over to the right side of his desk, his action final. "As soon as Nathan's police contact saw the painting on the wall in that photo you took of Banks, he said that Nathan's right. It appears to be from a museum collection that was stolen six months ago. I know you told Banks he could see a proof of the interview today, but you need to tell him we got held up and you'll get it to him in a couple of days. The police don't want him seeing the photo and spooking him. That should give the police enough time to investigate."

"You mean give them enough time for a surprise raid of his home!" I snap. "Look, I don't know if he's guilty or not—for all we know it's a very good replica—but my reputation is on the line here, Stan. I promised Banks the only reason I was there was to interview him. He'll never believe a police shake down the day after I interviewed him wasn't my plan all along." My heart thumps erratically with my worry. My boss and Nathan have no clue about Sebastian's past connection to Banks and I certainly won't be sharing that info with the Tribune, but coming down on Banks would be like kicking a hornet's nest and turning it on the Blakes.

"Calm down, Talia. If the painting really is from that collection, then this is for the greater good. And honestly, that's what your job is supposed to be about anyway, not fluff articles."

"Good investigative work," Nathan chimes in as he moves to stand next to me. "Remember, that's what we do here."

"I prefer *ethical* investigative work." I glare at him, folding my arms. "After this, my 'word' won't mean anything."

I pivot and start toward his door. "Where are you going?" Stan calls, tension in his tone. "We need to discuss upcoming projects."

"For a late lunch. Rest assured your duplicitous message will be conveyed."

I leave his office and march straight toward mine. Nathan's so close behind me I can smell his cologne.

"Talia, wait up."

I stop in my doorway and block his entrance. "I don't know what your problem is, Nathan, but you just put me at risk."

"I insisted that the police have to find some other reason to get into the house. That way it can't be traced back to us. You're worrying too much."

"Are you really that naive? Banks may seem easy going, but he's not the kind of guy you cross. Once the police zero in on that painting, Banks will blame the only investigative journalist who's recently been allowed an exclusive interview in his home."

Nathan slides his hands into his pockets and rocks on his heels, his expression confident. "I guarantee you that Banks has made many enemies over the years. You're probably the last person who'll enter his mind."

"*Good journalists* don't bank on probabilities," I snap.

He lowers his arms, tension edging into his stance. "I was there too. He could easily blame me instead."

"Well, that makes me feel so much better."

"If he tries to come after you, he'll regret it, Talia." Gaze hardening, he crosses his arms. "With Banks's history, I could dig up so much dirt on the guy I could bury him."

My ex has done some things on a professional level that I've wanted to choke him for in the past, but listening to him now makes my stomach churn. This reckless and aggressive behavior is something I've never seen in him before. "What has gotten into you lately?"

His brown gaze sharpens, his jaw hardening. "You should've married me, Talia. I can protect you just as well as Mr. Ex-Military."

"That's what forcing me to go back on my word with Banks is all about? Who I'm with?"

"I didn't put that painting on that guy's wall. And the old Talia wouldn't have let it slide either, but my point is I'll protect you." Stepping closer, he lowers his voice. "For fucks sake, I took two bullets for you, Talia. If that doesn't say I never stopped caring…I don't know what does."

My face heats with guilt over Hayes shooting him. I've seen Nathan wince and roll his shoulder from time to time. "You don't need to prove anything to me, Nathan. We're work colleagues, nothing more."

His jaw tightens. "You came to the hospital. You care, Talia."

"I wanted to make sure you were all right. I felt horrible that you got caught in the crossfire of Hayes' vendetta against me. But you mistook human decency for something more. I'm happily married, Nathan. You need to move on."

Before he can say anything else, I walk into my office and shut the door, ending the conversation. As angry as I am at him for this Banks's situation, Nathan's partially right about one thing. I don't view things as black and white as I used to, but then again, I have more than myself to worry about now. I have a family to protect, too.

Sitting down, I immediately dial the number I have for Banks. I'm pretty sure it's the house's landline—the guy's that private. My hands shake as I wait for him to answer. Once it goes to voicemail, I leave the message Stan asked me to convey, then hang up and type Stan an email. Once I hit Send, I bite my lip and try to decide what to do next.

For all I know, the police could raid Banks's house today. The last thing I want is for the Blakes to suffer any kind of blowback from this. I cooperated as far as the police are concerned, but how can I still honor my word with Banks? It's not as if I wouldn't go hard after the guy if he later became part of a Tribune investigation, but in this particular case, my word is who I am. My gaze lands on the flyer for a brand new pizza delivery place in my inbox, and I quickly grab the paper and my purse before I head down the backstairs, hoping like hell this new place delivers to the Lower East Side.

As I'm rushing to my car, the last person I expect to see is my aunt.

"Talia, I was just coming up to see you, dear," she calls from across the lot as I reach my car.

She seems a bit wound up, which puts me instantly on alert. All I can think about is her fighting with my father yesterday and then my father asking me to give her a second chance. The dual imagery is making my stomach roil. "Aunt Vanessa I have an appointment that I really need to keep. Could this possibly wait until later?"

She twists her purse's straps around her hands. "I'm sure you're busy with decisions and check lists and such, but since you haven't left any voice messages this past week, I thought I'd be the one to open the lines of communication, so I came to you."

What is she talking about? "I haven't called."

"Oh..." The look of disappointment on her face makes the invitation in my purse suddenly feel like a cinderblock. This would be the perfect time to invite her. Before I can tamp down my apprehension enough to speak, her expression tenses. "Well, in that case, then I do have something to talk to you about. I'd like to hire BLACK Security. I know a word from you will help smooth the path."

She shifted gears so fast, I blink in surprise. "Why do you want to hire Sebastian?"

"I think someone's watching me," my aunt says in a whisper after she glances behind her.

"There's no one there," I say, pursing my lips. The parking lot behind her is empty. Is she messing with me? How many times has she manipulated my life and relationships in the past? Were there more than the ones I'm aware of?

"They're not there now," she says, bristling. "This has

been going on for a couple of weeks. I want someone I can trust to take on my case."

"I'm so glad you feel he's *trustworthy*."

"Of course I do. He saved your life. That's all that matters in my book."

My sarcasm completely flew over my aunt's head. She's serious. And now she's trying to drag my husband into her twisted web, which will in turn include me. What new angle is she playing? I can't deal with not knowing her agenda, but I definitely won't allow her to rope Sebastian into whatever plan she's concocting. That invitation in my purse is going straight into the trash. "I'm sorry, but you'll have to hire another firm to help you, Aunt Vanessa. There are tons of reputable ones out there. I really need to go now."

"But...Talia." She reaches for my arm. "I'd really like to work things out. I miss being a part of your life. Seeing you get married would be such a highlight."

"I miss *trusting* you implicitly. And I don't know that I ever will again."

The hurt on her face makes me feel like a royal bitch. I've never been so blunt with my aunt, but she needs to understand how much damage she caused and I need to focus on mending other relationships right now. Pulling free of her hold, I shut the door and drive off to save the Blakes from a mess I created.

CHAPTER SEVEN

Sebastian

$\mathcal{M}$y steps slow as I leave the jewelers with a wedding gift for Talia. Banks is leaning against my car, arms crossed. My whole frame tenses, but I force myself not to immediately rush the asshole. He had to have followed me from the BLACK Security office. "What are you doing here?" I don't bother with small talk. I want him the fuck away from my world. The fact he even crossed into my domain infuriates me.

Banks doesn't move from his position. Instead he leans on the car even more and rubs his goatee, his dark eyes studying me in slow, calculating sweeps. "You know, I thought you had something to do with that raid on my warehouse a while back, but I couldn't prove it." Pushing off my car, he gets in my face, his eyes narrowed to slits, teeth bared. "The next time you want to go toe-to-toe with me, have the balls to do it yourself. Don't send your woman to do your backdoor dirty work for you like some kind of sniveling bitch."

Before he can step back, I grab his shoulder in a painful hold and extend my arm, forcing him away from me on my terms. "It was a fucking interview, Banks. Don't put your paranoia on me or my family. Though, I see it was a mistake for Talia to believe you were interview-worthy. You haven't changed one bit."

"Protecting my own is always my priority." Banks winces in pain, then yanks out of my vise hold. Rubbing his shoulder, he growls, "My *paranoia* showed up at my door two hours ago with a search warrant, looking to get my ass arrested. I don't believe in coincidences." He takes a step back, just out of my reach. "For the record, after turning me down as a punk teen, you only lived because I didn't think you were a threat. Don't make me see you that way now, Blackie. You want your past to stay there? Don't pull it forward and sure as shit don't fuck with it. I've got a lot more to protect and I'm far less forgiving in my old age."

I step forward, my fists clenched to keep from pounding the asshole into the cement. There are too many cameras on the street and the last thing I need is an assault charge the day before my wedding. "You really think you're worth my time?" I look him up and down with pent-up loathing and stop short of spitting at his feet. "Stay the hell away from me and mine, Banks. If I wanted to destroy you, trust me...by the time you saw me coming the ground under your feet would already be gone. Off the top of my head, I can think of ten ways to pull you apart. Every facet of your life would crumble, from family to funds. Now get the fuck out of my face before my restraint disappears and the first facet you feel is my fist smearing you all over the street."

Banks folds his arms and puffs up his chest. "You've been warned. You're not the only person with friends in high and low places, Blackie. Remember that."

His veiled threat delivered, Banks slides his hands in his pockets and strolls down the road, whistling.

My phone's at my ear before Banks turns the corner. "What's Talia's status, Theo?"

"She popped into a pizza place for lunch and brought me out a slice, then headed to her publishers. Been at Midtown Central a little over an hour. What's up? You sound tense."

What's she doing at her publisher? "I've got a lot on my mind."

"Wedding jitters?"

Normally his nosiness would annoy the hell out of me. Today, I could use a little levity to keep from overreacting. I don't want to say anything to raise the alarm just yet, so I snort. "Something like that. Keep a close eye and send updates."

"You worried she won't show?" Theo says, chuckling.

"You trying to get fired?"

I hang up and immediately text Talia.

You didn't mention going to Midtown today.

Checking up on me, are you?

Theo's smartass comment seems apt, so I smirk and reply.

Just making sure you're not running for the hills.

Nah, I take the "'Til death do us part" very seriously.

Sounds like an opening line of a new T.A. Lone book. Is that why you were at Midtown?

Yep, I just signed a new contract for two more books.

I frown. The Tribune kept her swamped so much she only had time to work on one book this year.

Are you sure you won't be overextending yourself with two books? I thought you were only going to contract one at a time.

Two books came to me fully formed. Jared wanted both.

Greedy bastard.

My editor gets books. You get me. Looks like you're both greedy bastards.

Fair warning. Tomorrow's contract will have ironclad evergreen clauses and non-competes out the ying-yang. I also plan to demand that Aaron White be the exclusive love interest in your fictional worlds. Be ready to sign on the dotted line, no addendums allowed.

Ha, you just want a guarantee you'll be invited to all the book signings.

I'll be there as your security anyway. Plus, your female readers adore me.

I do all the work and you get the adoration. Hmm, seems a bit out of balance.

I grin that she's in good spirits.

How's it my fault that you've made Aaron White one hot badass? Theo is your shadow today. For my sanity, keep it that way.

Love you too, Mr. Eye-Candy. See you at home at three.

Banks said his peace and I said mine. Extra security will be assigned at the rehearsal. I refuse to worry Talia with this. The last thing she should be feeling is guilt the day before her wedding. I pull her gift from my pocket and slide my finger across the stones. Not that I'll ever admit it to Cass, but marrying Talia again in front of our families and friends was absolutely the right call.

CHAPTER EIGHT

Talia

"*What* are you doing here? You haven't lost the bet already, have you?" Cass laughs as she walks into our old apartment while I'm vacuuming dust bunnies left behind after I rolled up the area rugs.

I turn off the machine and glance around at the progress I've made. "No, I was just here to collect some old contract paperwork and the dust was getting to me."

Cass gestures to the wet bucket and bathroom cleaning supplies. "The bathrooms were getting to you too?" Folding her arms, she taps her foot. "What gives, Talia? You only clean out of the blue when you're upset. Don't tell me that your husband's making you reconsider this remarriage?"

I lean on the vacuum and shake my head. I don't

want to talk about the mistake I made with Banks. I can only hope my note in the pizza box warning him about a potential raid got to him in time. "Sebastian and I are good. It's just work related stuff." Perking up, I smile. "Oh, but I did just sign a two-book contract today, so that's technically reason to celebrate."

Cass narrows her gaze. "You're not distracting me with shiny new things. What's going on?"

Hopefully the Banks thing is resolved, but there is one thing she needs to know. Sighing, I tug her over to the couch. "My aunt won't be coming to the wedding, Cass."

"Why not? she asks, completely confused.

I push my sweaty hair back from my face and blow out a breath. "I never told you about my past, but for you to understand *why*, you'll have to know the history."

Cass's eyes widen several times while I relay the story about my life as a teen and about Hayes, Walt, and Amelia, and how I got forced into delivering drugs after Hayes violated me when I was a teen.

"That's why shutting down that drug ring in college was so important to you," she whispers, tears glistening in her eyes as she reaches over and clasps my hands.

"Yes, the only reason I didn't push my aunt for us to leave that awful situation back then was because of Amelia. Since her mother abandoned her and Walt was knee-deep in making drugs, Aunt Vanessa and I were the only true family that little girl had. I needed to keep her safe so she wouldn't have to go through what I did when she grew older."

Tears fall as I tell her how Amelia died, about the explosion my aunt set off that destroyed our apartment, and how that was the night I first met Sebastian. "My aunt also later hired that girl to break Nathan and me up because she didn't believe we were right together."

Cass shakes her head through my story, her glassy eyes full of sympathy. Her supportive silence gives me the boost I need to continue on. I leave out the part about Isabel hiring Hayes all those years ago to take out Sebastian. That's Sebastian's secret to reveal, not mine.

"I can't believe how yours and Sebastian's lives have crossed."

I smile, thinking about the many times he saved me, then sigh. "That's a very long way of telling you why I won't be inviting my aunt. Sadly, my side of the church will be sparsely populated, but I just can't trust Aunt Vanessa. I've kept my distance, but she even approached me today trying to reconnect. When I didn't respond, she then told me she wanted to hire BLACK Security because she thinks she's being followed." I exhale and shake my head. "Ugh, I told her I had to go. I just couldn't deal, Cass. I haven't been able to get over how she risked my safety in the past and then later tried to control who I ended up with in my future."

"I'm sorry, Talia." Cass leans close and hugs me tight.

"Your side of the church will be just as full. *I'm* your family. We might not share blood, but our bond is unbreakable. I love you and will always have your back. Thank you for trusting me enough to share about your past. So many things make sense now."

Leaning back, she clasps my shoulders. "And for the record, though you probably don't want to hear this...I think your aunt does love you. She might have a twisted way of showing it, but the sun, moon and stars shine in her world because of you. I've seen it every time she says your name."

I frown at her. "You're not making this decision easy."

Cass shrugs. "I won't lie just to make you feel better, but I do understand your need to take a step back from Vanessa. Your wounds are too fresh right now, so if not having her attend lets you breathe easier, then I support your decision. This is your wedding day, not hers."

When I offer a shaky smile, she releases me, her gaze narrowing slightly. "Okay, so tell me the part you've been holding back."

I give her a puzzled look. "I just revealed all kinds of personal stuff."

"Which I appreciate, but you're not getting away with avoiding telling me what happened at work. You need a clean conscience for tonight, girl."

Tucking my damp hair behind my ears, I blow out an unsteady breath. "I quit today."

Cass's eyes bug. "Why? What happened?"

I quickly tell her about the Banks fiasco and my effort to fix it, making sure to leave out his connection to Sebastian's past. "Between having to go back on my word, and then being forced to find a way around it to keep a shred of my integrity, I'm just done. I have too much to lose now just to pursue a story."

"That's why you went straight to your editor and signed a two book contract," Cass says with a smug look as she folds her arms. "What did Sebastian say?"

"He doesn't know that I quit." I squeeze her arm. "And you can't tell him."

"Do you plan to hide out here while you're supposed to be at work, forever?"

I smirk at her smartass comment. "No, I want to go work for BLACK Security. I'm a damn good investigator and Sebastian knows it, but for some reason he's being stubborn. Maybe he doesn't want to see me everyday at home and at work. Maybe he thinks we'll fight. I don't know, but the last thing I want him to do is hire me like this." I cross my arms and set my jaw. "I don't want to be asked to join his team out of a sense of obligation."

"Are you serious?" Cass snorts. "That man adores you, Talia."

"That's the problem. He'll ignore his reservations and ask me to come to BLACK Security just to make me happy."

Cass rolls her eyes. "Since when has Sebastian Quinn Blake ever done anything he didn't *want* to do?"

I immediately think of Sebastian refusing to turn Isabel in to the police for her part in his mother's murder. "When it comes to family, his stubborn streak bends, Cass. I've told you this in confidence. Swear to me that you won't tell Calder. I don't want it getting back to Sebastian."

Cass draws an X across her chest. "I promise, but you can't keep this from him for long. He's too perceptive. He'll know something is off."

"I know. I just want a bit more time to figure things out."

"You could always write full time?"

I shake my head. "If writing was all I did, I would miss the rush of investigating. Life experiences fuel my muse, and when you're writing suspense and mystery...that's an unusual 'well' that needs refilling."

Tapping the tip of her nose, Cass nods. "I gotcha. While waiting for my New York book to release, I've been trying to figure out a way to merge my passion for photography and publishing. Jared wants more books, but he needs another mock up. After the wedding is over, I'm going to sit down and brainstorm ideas."

"Cass! Why didn't you tell me? I don't want my wedding stuff to keep you from work."

"*Pshaw*! I'm enjoying this. Ideas are percolating while I help you tie the knot the way you *should've* the first time.

Maybe I'll run my thoughts on projects by you when you get back from your honeymoon in Spain." She exhales a nostalgic sigh. "You're going to love every bit of it, Talia."

"With the amazing itinerary you put together for places to stay and things to do, how can I not enjoy it?" Inspiration hits and I snap my fingers. "Oooh, Cass! What about travel books? One for each major city you've visited? You're so organized with your checklists. You've been so many places, eaten at such fabulous restaurants...and your photos of the food and the breathtaking scenery... holy cow! I'm excited just thinking about it. Jared and William will both love it!"

"Do you think so?" Cass's eyes light up. "I have so many wonderful memories and tons of amazing photos I've never used."

I nod. "I think Midtown would flip for something like that. And I'll be happy to help you proof them once they're written. It'll be my way of vicariously going on those trips with you."

Cass laughs, her smile extra wide. "I'm so excited, but for now...wedding rehearsal. I'm grabbing the tote bag I came for so I can keep all my paperwork in order tonight, and *you* need to get back and change. As your wedding planner, it's my duty to remind you that your limo will arrive to drive you to rehearsal in two hours."

"After a quick shower here, I'll pick up Sebastian's gift and then head home to change."

Cass's tote bag bumps against my hip as she hugs me before she leaves. "This is going to be an amazing wedding, Talia. Bringing friends and family together. I hope…well, I hope that I can convince Calder to invite Ben to our wedding. I want all our family there."

"Do you think Ben would come?" I ask. "I mean… considering that he wanted to marry you too."

Cass tucks her hair behind her ear. "Yeah, I think he would. Ben knows I love Calder…and honestly, I think he wants a relationship with his half-brother, but Calder has—"

"Trust issues? I know, but don't worry, we'll think of a way to get them talking." Smiling, I tug her bag's straps higher up on her shoulder. "Thank you for being the best wedding planner ever."

After Cass leaves, I hop in the shower and dry off, then frown at my neck in the mirror. It looks so bare without my Two Lias necklace. I quickly dress, then walk into the living room to retrieve it from the coffee table. I'd taken it off while cleaning so I wouldn't sweat all over it. It's not on the table, where I'd left it, so I start looking all around for it. Frustrated, I unroll the carpets and even take the vacuum apart after checking its bag, but I still don't find it. With an hour and fifteen minutes to run my errand and get dressed before rehearsal, I reluctantly give up my search and collect my paperwork and purse, before heading out.

Our penthouse apartment is quiet when I walk in.

Sebastian immediately pokes his head out of our bedroom doorway, his hair still damp from the shower. "I was getting worried. I thought for sure you would've been here getting dressed well before me. Come help me decide on a suit."

I follow him into the room and pull a box from the store bag on my arm. "Why don't you let this help you decide?"

His handsome face lights up as he reaches for the box. "What is it?"

"A surprise you don't have to wait to see. Open it."

When he lifts the dress shirt from the box, then quickly glances down at the space near the tail in surprise, I know he's wondering how I got Teresa to already add the tag that tell him the shirt color and the numbering system as to which ties and suits it coordinates with. I grin as he reads the special label I had added to this shirt.

"Color: ? See Talia."

His intrigued look makes me smile. "The material is wrinkle-free and is incredibly comfortable even starched, but the gift has another intent. At least once every couple of weeks, I want you to depend on me for something. Whenever you wear this shirt, I'll help you decide on a tie and suit to go with it."

"You're not going to tell me what color it is?"

When I shake my head, Sebastian runs his finger over the label, his gaze locked on the words. He's so quiet I'm not sure how he feels about it. "It was just a thought. If you'd rather I have Teresa add your usual color-coded label...."

He hooks his muscular arm around my shoulders and pulls me close, whispering against my temple. "I love it, Talia." Lifting up the shirt, he continues, "Want to help me pick out the tie?"

After I find the perfect tie and suit to go with the shirt, I wait until he's buttoned his pants, then I slide off my ring and hold it out to him.

"What are you doing? Put it back on."

I ignore his scowl of disapproval. "You'll do that tomorrow during the ceremony."

He lifts my left hand, his frown deepening as he runs his thumb over my naked ring finger. "I don't like not seeing it on your hand."

I take my ring, and as I tuck it into his pants' pocket, I kiss his jaw. "I'll be sleeping in your bed tonight anyway, Mister Black."

He cups the back of my neck, his hold tight. Sliding his thumb down the side of my throat with just enough pressure to make my body hum to life, he rumbles, "Don't think for one minute I'll make it easy for you to keep up this chaste ruse, Little Red. Not after watching you walk around all night without my ring on your finger. I don't give a damn that it's our rehearsal."

I rest my hand on his bare chest but can't make myself move away. Instead, I lean into his hard body and soak up his warmth. "You know I'm yours."

He trails his fingers down my back. Even through my clothes my skin prickles. Cupping my ass with a possessive hold, he pulls me against his erection and slides his mouth along my throat. "From those gorgeous red roots to the tips of your succulent toes, I'll spend every day reminding you why that's always going to be true."

"Is that part of your vows?" I whisper, amazed that he can still make me breathless with just words.

"No hints, Miss Nosey." Flashing a smile, he smacks my ass with a firm hand, making me tingle all the way to my toes. "Now go get dressed so we can get to the best part."

"Where I say, 'I do'?"

"No, *bed*," he says on a primal rumble.

His blue gaze sparking with determined, erotic intent makes the one dark brown spot in his left eye stand out. That beautiful mark sends my stomach into a tailspin and my nipples ache for the heat of his mouth. Chances of me withstanding Sebastian in unleashed seduction mode will be about as effective as an umbrella in a monsoon.

Shit.

My virtuous resolve is so completely screwed.

Once we arrive at the church in our separate limos, Sebastian says he needs to discuss a work issue with

Calder, so Cass and I leave the men talking in the church's entryway. The moment we walk into the church and she doesn't immediately see the pastor, Cass looks at her watch and mutters, "He insisted on our prompt arrival. Where is he?"

When she taps her foot and stares at her watch once more, my gaze strays to the lady walking a young teen girl to the front of the church. "We're here a bit early, Cass. Pastor Meyer is probably in his office."

"Ah, you're probably right. I'll go find him and let him know that we arrived on time."

"Who knew you were such a rule follower?" I tease.

Cass blows me a kiss before she heads back out of the church. Once the heavy doors close behind her, a hush descends on the otherwise empty space. I feel like I'm an intruder into this woman and young girl's prayer time. I sit in the last pew as they enter the first. As they kneel on the padded bench, then bow their heads in prayer, the imagery of flickering candles and scent of lemon floor wax suddenly transports me back to that awful night our apartment exploded.

My feet hurt from walking for what seemed like hours. No shelters would take us for the night. They were all full. It had started to rain again just when my jeans had nearly dried, but at least Blackie's jacket kept me warm. I was surprised that Aunt Vanessa didn't ask me about the leather coat swallowing me up, but she was so distracted trying to find us a place to sleep—and

*probably still in shock over losing Walt, Amelia, and everything
we owned—that she wasn't paying much attention to details.
I'm sure she was just so thankful I wasn't in our gape-holed
apartment full of fire and smoke.*

*The rain picked up and my aunt quickly tugged me into the
closest open building. I thought we would just stand inside the
church's main door, our shoes dripping onto the newly polished
wood floor as we waited the rain out. Instead, Aunt Vanessa
grabbed my hand and led me straight down the main aisle in the
empty church, directing me into the first pew.*

*My aunt wasn't a religious woman. I could count on two
hands the number of times I'd seen the inside of a church—
usually either an Easter or Christmas service. But tonight she
must've felt the need for spiritual guidance, so I kneeled with
her, bent my head, and closed my eyes.*

*While my aunt mumbled prayers for our future, I didn't
wish for a roof over our heads, nor did I begrudge losing all our
worldly possessions. In that safe, quiet place with smells of lemon
and burning candles, I hoped Amelia heard my tears for her loss,
said my thanks to the heavens for severing my connection to
Hayes, and I wished that one day I'd see Blackie again so that I
could thank him for saving me from myself. Would I even be in
that church beside my aunt if he hadn't come along?*

The woman and girl lift their heads from prayer,
drawing me back to the present. She wraps her arm around
the girl's shoulder and seems to be comforting her, much
like my aunt tried to do back then.

Of course, knowing what I do now—that Aunt Vanessa intentionally blew up the apartment—gives me a whole other perspective on the truths of that night.

Once the ladies stand and leave, with nothing to focus on, I stare at the massive cross on the far sanctuary wall and think about the selfless forgiveness and second chance it represents. My thoughts segue to my father's advice and the sudden ache in my chest is so strong, I have to take a couple of deep breaths.

We didn't just lose everything that night...my aunt destroyed it all. She could've packed a bag, hidden some things away before she blew up our apartment, but she didn't. She nuked everything to save me from having to face murder charges. Shooting Walt was an accident, but the rage in my heart that night for his part in Ameila's death wasn't. What would've happened if Aunt Vanessa hadn't done what she did? As extreme as her actions were, she did what she felt was the best thing for me. I blink back tears of self-doubt as I continue to stare at the cross.

"What's wrong, Talia?"

Sebastian slips into the pew beside me and wraps his arm around my shoulders, pulling me close. His warmth feels so good, I lean into him and swipe the wetness from my face.

"I don't know if I've made the right decision not inviting my aunt to the wedding."

"I thought you decided to invite her?"

I consider telling him about my aunt's visit earlier today, but instead tell him how I'm feeling. "I'm torn. She raised me, Sebastian. But I don't want our lives disrupted by some crazy new idea she might get. And I sure don't want you dragged into it either."

"I have no issues putting your aunt in her place whenever necessary, Talia. Worry for me should never enter your mind."

His assurance lifts the heaviness from my chest. "I don't know about the future, but it feels spiteful not to invite her. And that's not who I am."

He cups my jaw and lifts my chin so I fully meet his gaze. "Your forgiving nature is one of your most admirable qualities, Talia. I won't deny that I will always question your aunt's motives, but just because you extend an invitation to your wedding doesn't mean that it has to apply going forward. Think of it as honoring the person who raised you."

I fold my hand over his on my jaw and smile. "Will you promise to always say the right thing for the next oh... seventy or so years?"

"Every time you get frustrated with me..." The corner of his lip hikes in a smirk. "I'm going to remind you that you said that, Little Red."

I exhale an amused snort that echoes loudly in the quiet church. Just as I snicker, someone clears her throat behind us. We turn to see the entire wedding party now gathered near the doors inside the church. Isabel is next to the pastor, her icy blue gaze focused on us as she sniffs her disapproval. "Please respect our church at all times, Talia."

Before Sebastian can blast his stepmother, Adam steps close to his wife and hooks his arm in hers. "We'll go find our seats and let this rehearsal get rolling so we can move on to the dinner you've planned, Isabel."

Adam lets his wife walk ahead, and as Sebastian and I stand, he pauses and smiles at my silk dress. "You look stunning in royal blue, Talia."

"Thank you," I say, knowing it was Adam's way of trying to apologize for his wife. My husband's hand flexes against my back, his fingers tugging on the silk material before he moves them to the ends of my curled, unbound hair. I glance his way to see him staring at the strands. I'm in awe that he has managed to keep his colorblindness to himself for so long, but I'm also sad that the only color he can see clashes with my hair color. I would wear the most stunning dresses and heels in red every day.

Clasping Sebastian's hand, I smile and tug him to the front of the church, our families falling into place behind us.

At the front, Pastor Meyer claps his hands. "Gavin and Damien. Please step forward." Once Sebastian's half-brothers comply, he points to places behind Sebastian. "The groomsmen will need to stand here. Be sure to leave a space for the best man." He quickly waves to Calder. "Come take your place, Calder."

Without being told, Cass moves into position as my maid of honor and Sebastian's sister Mina steps into place behind her as my bridesmaid.

As Josi begins to fuss in her mother's arms, Isabel stands from the pew with an annoyed huff and approaches her daughter. "I'm assuming you have a sitter lined up, Mina?" she comments as she takes her granddaughter from Mina.

"Josi will attend the wedding," Sebastian cuts in, nodding his approval to his sister.

Adam instantly takes Josi from Isabel as she returns to her seat and bounces his granddaughter on his knee.

"Where's the father of the bride?" Pastor Meyer calls out, glancing around.

"I'm here. Traffic was extra heavy today." My father steps through the open door and quickly walks down the aisle toward us. "Three different men checked my ID outside. Now that's some tight security."

I look at Sebastian with a questioning gaze as Pastor Meyer says to Kenneth, "Please allow ample time for traffic tomorrow, Mr...?"

"It's Kenneth McAdams, Pastor, and I'll be sure to be here extra early."

My husband's unapologetic stare doesn't surprise me, so I shift my gaze to my father who just shrugs off the hassle with a jovial grin and hooks his arm in a formal pose, encouraging me to step into place beside him.

"Ready for this, Tally-girl?"

Sebastian's eyebrow hikes at the nickname, but otherwise my husband's expression remains stoic as my father and I start down the aisle toward the back of the church. I smile and nod to acknowledge Den standing off to the left. He must've entered right after my father did.

"I don't see your aunt here. Did you decide not to invite her?" my father asks in a low voice meant just for me.

"Actually I just decided before you arrived. I'm not sure how things will progress in the future, but she deserves to be here for this. I have her invitation in my purse. Would you do me a favor and deliver it to her?"

He smiles and pats my hand on his arm. The kindness in his green gaze makes my heart swell. Did my "forgiving" gene come from him? "I'll be happy to, Talia." Turning me around at the back of the church, he looks at me with pride. "Ready?"

I nod and exhale before we take the first step forward.

After three practice rounds, the pastor deems us ready for tomorrow. Cass's parents are waiting in the church's main entrance, along with Theo and two other men from BLACK Security.

Isabel walks briskly out of the church's main doors

with Den taking long strides to stay with her. She's talking harshly into her phone. "That's not what I requested. Fix it right now or I will make sure no one in my social circle uses your restaurant again." A pause. "Unacceptable. You listen to me…"

As Isabel exits through the church's propped open main doors, Den takes up a post on the threshold, his ever-watchful gaze shifting between Isabel and the Blake family inside the church. Cass moves to my side and mutters under her breath, "Looks like the Dragon Lady is raining fire down on the poor commoners. We'll all either have the best meal ever, or go home with the worst case of revenge diarrhea because of her."

"It'll be fine, Cass," I say, snickering at her comment. I nod to Calder, appreciating that he's taking the time to introduce my father to Cass's parents. My heart feels full when I see Adam call Gavin and Damian over to where he's standing beside Sebastian. The moment the brothers join them, good-natured ribbing commences with Sebastian taking the brunt of it. He barks out a laugh and I smile, hoping I feel this happily content tomorrow.

Mina walks up with a tear-stained Josi holding an animal cracker. "I'm sorry Josi got fussy, Talia. Of course Mom reminded me that I must be better prepared to calm her tomorrow during the ceremony. I promise I'll have extra distractions on hand for my parents while I'm standing up there with you and Sebastian."

I touch Josi's rosy cheek and smile when she tries to share her cracker with me. "Don't worry, Mina. Josi's a delight and everyone understands little ones can get fussy."

"But my mom—"

"Is anxious about the dinner." I gesture to Isabel pacing outside. "Don't let her get to you. I don't."

Cass follows my line of sight and stiffens next to me. "She wouldn't *dare*."

"What?" Mina and I say at the same time.

"Your mother is heading for Talia and Sebastian's limo," Cass says to Mina. "She's the one who suggested that I put that red ribbon on the limo's mirror to distinguish it from the others. How can she not see it?" She glances at me. "You and Sebastian must leave for the restaurant before the rest."

"Mom wouldn't do that," Mina says as she bends to pick up the cracker piece Josi dropped on the floor.

"She's just gotten in the car." Cass huffs. "This is completely unacceptable. It's the top of the line limo. I need to go deal with this."

Cass heads for the open doorway, and as Calder walks over to meet her, a questioning look on his face, I see the limo move ahead a few feet, presumably to wait for traffic. Once the vehicle pulls into the line of cars, I call after Cass, "It's fine. We'll just take the other limo to the restaurant."

A shockingly loud boom makes my heart jump and my

ears hurt, but the sight of Den stumbling to the side and Cass falling back against Calder at the entrance spurs me into action, my heart pounding. I run over to see if she's okay and exhale my relief when Den nods to let me know he's fine.

Calder quickly turns Cass around and clasps her face in a tight hold. "Are you okay?"

She's pale and shaken but she nods and wraps her arms around his waist, hugging him tight. "My ears are ringing."

Den's got his phone to his ear and my heart jerks when I hear him say, "There's been an explosion."

Where did it come from?

Giving the address to the police, Den holds his hand up to silently tell Adam and family to say back, and that's when I see the raging fire and smoke billowing out of the back of the limo.

Oh God!

As Den hangs up, then runs out of the church to get closer to the flaming car, Mina quickly rushes to my side, confusion and alarm on her face. The moment she sees the fire raging in the limo, she screams and Josi begins to wail. I sense Mina tensing, poised to bolt into pursuit, and I immediately put my arm out, blocking her from running out of the church.

"Stop, Mina! The car might explode again. You can't risk yourself or Josi by going anywhere near it," I say in a shaky voice.

Mina gestures wildly, her eyes wide and tears rolling down her face. "Mom's in the car! We have to help her!"

Sebastian, Adam, Gavin, and Damien just join us near the entrance of the church as Mina calls out about her mom. Horror and disbelief crosses their tense faces, and all the Blake men burst into action.

"Lock down the perimeter," Sebastian calls to his BLACK Security men already standing in the street. Turning back toward us, he says, "Theo, on Talia!"

"Already here," the big guy grunts his agreement from directly behind me. I want to look back and acknowledge Theo, but I'm too worried for the driver and Isabel.

The fire's too hot for the men to get close to the back of the limo, but Sebastian calls, "The driver's out cold. Get me something to break the window." Calder quickly approaches with a crowbar Gavin gets from one of the limo drivers. After they knock out the window, Sebastian says to one of the BLACK Security men, "Throw me your knife; the seatbelt's jammed!"

Hurry! My throat closes with worry that the fire consuming the back half of the limo could shift forward at any moment toward the men or cause another explosion.

The warm night air moves in greasy heat waves around them as Sebastian catches the pocketknife thrown his way and quickly cuts the seatbelt away. Sweat from the heat beads on their faces as Sebastian and Calder haul the guy out, then Damien and Gavin take over and carry the unconscious driver across the street to safety. I exhale my relief that they were successful, but my heart breaks for Adam. He slowly sinks down on the stairs, his hands jammed in his hair. All he can do is watch the fire burn, completely helpless to stop it.

As a car farther down the street pulls away, tires screeching, the sound draws Sebastian's attention. Den throws his keys to my husband. "At least get the license plate. My BMW is the last car behind the limos. I've got it covered here."

Fisting his hand around the keys, Sebastian locks gazes with his cousin. "With me, Cald."

Once Calder leaves with Sebastian, Cass moves to my side and I realize that her parents and my father have joined us too. Hooking her arm around my waist, Cass's voice is tense with worry. "I can't believe this is happening."

Too shocked to speak, I put my arm around Mina's shoulders and tug her to my other side, folding Josi between us and into the protective circle of our family just as the faint whine of fire truck sirens sounds in the distance.

Mina's blonde hair sways with the slow shake of her head. Anguish creasing her face, her lips tremble in a quiet whisper, "They're too late, Talia. My mom is gone."

CHAPTER NINE

Sebastian

$\mathcal{M}_y$ whole body is strung tight as I start the BMW. I don't even wait for Calder to fully shut his door before I gun the engine and shoot into traffic, taking off after the car that squealed away in the darkness.

Calder grabs the dash and mutters, "Fucking hell, Bash!" as he pulls his door closed. The second his hand is free, he points ahead, barking, "There! Do you see him? Four cars ahead."

I shift gears and weave around two cars, gaining on the sports car speeding away. Thankfully the traffic isn't bumper to bumper, but it's enough to make keeping a constant eye on the car difficult as more cars merge onto the road from side streets.

I zoom through the next light and Calder jerks a

surprised gaze my way. "Where are you going? He just turned down that side street."

"No, he didn't. He's three cars ahead," I snap.

Calder leans to the side trying to see around the traffic. "That's the wrong car, Bash."

"It's the right one," I insist, my hands gripping the wheel tight.

"That's a white Mustang. The one we're after is light blue." Frowning, Calder points to the road ahead. "Take that next left and hopefully we can cut him off."

Frustrated with myself, the wheels squeal as I take a sharp turn and hit the pedal to make up time down the side street.

A Mustang zooms past right as I reach the crossroad, and I immediately turn to follow it. Jamming my foot to the floor, I curse the lack of streetlights on this road.

"Can you read the license plate?" I growl.

Calder leans forward and squints. "It's nine-nine-six, I think. It's too dark to make out the letters."

"The light's changing ahead. We'll get the fucker!"

When we're within a couple car lengths from the Mustang, another car pulls from a side alleyway, its front end blocking our pursuit of the sports car.

The Mustang blows through the yellow light and I lay on the horn at the girl with a bob haircut and bright red lipstick. She shrugs and flips me off before straightening her car with its unicorn hood ornament in front of mine just as the light turns red.

"Sonofabitch!" I slam my hand against the steering wheel. As I pull my phone out and dial Elijah, Calder kicks off his shoe, then hands me his sock.

"Bind your wound. You're bleeding all over Den's car."

Grunting, I glance down and see I have a gash on the side of my hand that's bleeding pretty bad. "Fucking hell," I mutter.

"Come again?" Elijah says.

Calder grabs my phone and puts it on speaker while I wrap his sock around my wound to stop the bleeding. "We need a DMV search."

I take my phone back and tell Elijah, "Run it for the following: Light blue Mustang, partial New York plate: nine-nine-six."

"Got it. Any other details?"

"That's all we—"

"Yeah," Calder cuts in, sliding a look my way. "It was one of those custom plates with the New York Knicks symbol on it."

"That'll narrow it some. I'll call you back."

As soon as I hit the End button, Calder says in a quiet tone, "What was that about?"

I can feel my cousin's gaze drilling into me, but I keep my focus on the road. Folding my hands on the wheel, I wince. Now that the rush of the chase is over, the pain in my hand is kicking in. "What was what about?" I grit through the sting and push on the gas once the light switches to the green position.

"How the hell did you mix up blue and white?"

"They're both light colors," I say in a tight tone, hating that my limited vision screwed us over tonight.

"You blanked on the Knicks symbol on the license plate too. It's not like you to miss details, Bash. Fucking ever. I've seen you remember details in the middle of a firefight, but tonight you missed both."

I curl my fingers tight on the wheel and welcome the shooting pain. "I'm colorblind, Cald."

"Since when? I've known you since we were teens."

When I shake my head, his silence makes me tense, but I refuse to look his way. "It happened on my last mission. A bomb went off, I took a hit, and when I woke in the hospital, the only color I could see was red. Otherwise everything is various shades of gray."

"How long have you been colorblind?"

"Years."

"How is that possible?" My cousin turns in the seat toward me. "If you can only see in shades of gray, then how in the hell did you defuse that bomb under that MMA ring?"

I cut a look his way. "Talia's nail clippers weren't the only tool I used that night."

"She told you the wire colors?"

Nodding, I roll to a stop at another light. "Be glad Talia

listened to her intuition that she needed to be at the fight that night or you and I might not be here."

"What the fuck, Bash!"

I exhale and roll my shoulders. "I'll disclose the truth about my sight to the whole BLACK Security team tonight. I'll never let my visual limitation put anyone I care about in danger again."

"Goddamnit, if you weren't driving I'd punch you square in the jaw. I don't give a rat's ass about the team right now. I'm pissed that you didn't tell *me*. Or was your speech about considering me your brother just bullshit to get me talking?"

"Family *always* matters," I grate, glaring at him just as the light turns green.

"Apparently only when it's convenient for you."

Surprised by the underlying hurt in his comment, I turn my attention back to the road. "It's hard enough to admit to myself that I'll never be in top form again, let alone share that with anyone else."

"Talia knows."

"And I'm sure you've shared things with Cass that you've never told me, but you deserve to know the one area your business partner will fall short, Cald."

"So we'll argue about colors. Big fucking deal." He snorts, waving his hand. "It's not like we're a couple of decorators. But the moment you can't tell the difference between dark and light beer whenever you lose a bet, then we'll have a problem."

I grunt, appreciating how much lighter I feel now that Calder knows. "Your prize of choice is safe."

My chest tightens all over again as I turn onto the road that leads back to the church. I feel for Mina. She'll be devastated by this. While Isabel's death is horrifically tragic, the danger her loss represents to the rest of the Blake family is my highest priority. *Was Isabel the target?* I wouldn't be surprised if I wasn't her only enemy; that woman's tiger stripes were tree-ring deep. But it's not lost on me that I could've been the target. My run in with Banks plays over in my mind as I consider that the limo *was* marked for Talia and me.

The moment the church comes into view, I'm relieved to see Den looking intimidating as hell as he glares at the two police officers standing in front of him just inside the church doors. And though I would prefer the safer scenario of my whole family behind the church's main doors, closed and locked, seeing Den flanking Talia's right and Theo standing between Talia and Cass, while the BLACK Security team not only holds the perimeter, but keeps the news crews away, my mind is eased a little. Talia glances our way, her heart-broken gaze following the BMW's arrival back on the scene. *Even when she's sad, she's beautiful. God, I fucking love every bit of her.*

What if I had stayed behind to double check security for the wedding tomorrow? The thought that I could've lost Talia if she'd driven off in that limo instead of Isabel makes me feel equally violent and nauseous. My siblings, Cass's parents and Talia's father are standing farther back in the church's entryway talking with two uniformed police officers. Now that the fire is doused, several firemen are swarming the wet, charred limo, trying to pry the damaged door off. I glance at Calder as I park in a spot across the street from the spectacle. At least the gawking news people are completely oblivious to our arrival.

"All non-critical BLACK Security assignments go on the back burner until we find the bastard who did this. After I brief the team on a possible lead—"

"You have something other than the Mustang driver?"

I talk over Calder's interruption. "We need to question the family to see if anything was going on with any of them or Isabel, any kind of threats that we didn't know about. Then we can assign a security detail to each family member to go with them for the night."

"We'll be stretched thin trying to cover everyone on top of our current client base."

I shake my head. "Two contracts are up in a couple of days. I'm going to request an early release due to exigent circumstances. Any client who reads the news will know the reason why."

"What lead, Bash?"

"A guy named Banks from Banks's Boys in my old neighborhood was a bit pissed about a raid the police did on his place and paid me a visit today. He assumed I was behind it, but I thought he was all bluff and bluster. I just want to make sure that's all it was."

"Jesus! You could've lead with that!"

"It could be nothing," I say, keeping my tone even.

Shaking his head, Calder stares intently at the crowd. "I know our guys have their hands full right now, but why the hell hasn't Den at least closed the family in?" My cousin echoes my thoughts as he cranes his neck to see around the crush of people. "Ah, now I see…your dad hasn't left the steps," he continues, the heat of anger leaving his tone. "I know Gavin and Damien will deal, but do you think your father and Mina will be okay?"

It's ironic that the one person who would care the most about the sensationalism the paparazzi will make of tonight's tragedy isn't here. Isabel would be beside herself worrying what the rags would print as to why this happened to our family. So long as no one's reputation is unjustly slandered, I don't give a damn. "The guys will be fine and my father will most likely bury himself in work. Mina…" Talia's comment about my sister being stronger than I give her credit for flickers through my mind. "She has us. Come on. It's time to convince Adam to move inside." I open the car door, not looking forward to plowing through the paparazzi to get to my family. "I want those damn church doors shut."

CHAPTER TEN

Talia

"*What* the hell is he doing here?"

"It's good to see you too, *brother*." Ben shakes his dark head and rises from our sofa as Sebastian, Calder, Cass, and I exit the elevator to our penthouse apartment.

"I called him." I shoot Calder a look, then smile at Ben. "Thank you for waiting inside. The less attention we draw, the better."

"I'm sorry for your loss," Ben says to all of us before he glances at the taped gauze on Sebastian's hand that's already showing signs of new blood. "Let's head into the kitchen and stop that bleeding."

Sebastian doesn't comment that I called Ben or asked him to wait inside. He'd seen my look of concern when he had to change the bandage twice at the church while he talked to our family. On the way home, my husband told me about his confrontation on the street with Banks, and then I told him about my pizza box attempt to warn Banks after Stan got the police involved.

While Ben and Sebastian move over to the kitchen table for him to stitch my husband up, Calder rounds on me, his green eyes flashing with anger. "You gave him the code to your apartment?"

"Yes, I did. I know you have issues trusting your half-brother, but he has proven that he can be trusted. The pool of people our family can truly depend on just got a lot smaller tonight, so dial it back."

Calder starts to speak, but Cass puts a hand on his arm. "We're all tense, but I'm too exhausted for the extra twenty minute drive home, so don't get us kicked out."

He grumbles an apology and folds her into his arms. Cass hugs his trim waist and gives me a secret smile around his shoulder.

Nodding my appreciation for her intervention, I sigh my exhaustion. "So no one had any skeletons in their closet but Sebastian and me with Banks?"

"Isabel could've had some, but we'll never know," Cass says as she turns in her fiancé's arms and leans back against his chest.

"Since the license plate turned out to belong to a completely different car, we can scratch that lead off our list," Calder says, folding his arms around Cass's stomach.

"Once I get a shower to wash away the sweat and soot from the fire, I'm good for another hour of brainstorming."

I blink through my exhaustion. The police questions were grueling enough, but then Sebastian and Calder drilled everyone, including Cass's parents and my father, with equal intensity for another hour. The stress of that on top of worrying I might've been responsible for Banks's retaliation is making me feel sick to my stomach.

Before I can speak, Cass puts her hand on my arm. "You look like you're about to fall over, Talia. I vote we go to bed and see what the investigators' reports say tomorrow." She looks at Calder. "I know the BLACK team will be all over this in the AM anyway. Whatever Talia and I can contribute once our brains aren't fried, we will."

Returning her gaze to me, she squeezes my arm. "There's at least one silver lining. Now your aunt has more time to get herself in your good graces."

"Did your aunt contact you?" Sebastian says, a frown creasing his brow as he flexes his hand with the new bandage wrapped fully around his palm.

"Be sure to keep that dry for a few days and get that antibiotic prescription filled." Ben approaches, snapping his doctor's kit closed.

Sebastian nods. "Will do. Thank you for coming, Ben."

"You're welcome." Ben smiles at Cass as he continues speaking, "You've got my number, so if you ever need me—"

"It's late. Good night, Ben," Calder says in a tight tone.

Ben shakes his head. "Difficult patients will cost double my usual fee."

"That's fair." Sebastian smirks. "It'll just come out of his check."

Calder glances between the two men. "Did you just hire him?"

Sebastian shrugs. "Rick retired and we need someone who's discrete."

"Don't I get any say-so in this personnel decision?" Calder asks.

"No," Sebastian and I answer at the same, our gazes locking in agreement.

"You could always stop doing things that require my expertise." Ben adopts a lighthearted tone as he walks over and enters the elevator.

When Calder just drills the back of his head with a hard stare, his brother turns in the elevator to face us. "That's what I thought. Until next time..."

The moment the elevators close, Sebastian faces me.

"Did she?" He frowns. "Is that why you were feeling guilty at the church?"

"No, that had nothing to do with it. She approached me earlier today and I was focused on taking care of the Banks thing. She said she wanted to hire BLACK Security after I didn't really respond to her attempt to chat. That's when my worry for her motives ramped and I turned her down for any help from your company before I left."

His blue eyes darken. "As far as she knew, Vanessa didn't think she was going to be invited to our wedding?"

I nod. "I only asked my father to give her the invitation tonight at the rehearsal."

Sebastian pulls out his phone and dials. "Hey, Elijah. I know it's late, but I want to add one more name to the list of potential threats: Vanessa Granger."

I shake my head the whole time he's on the phone. The moment he hangs up, I stare at him with wide eyes. "You don't think she's capable of this, do you?"

"We have to eliminate her as a potential threat."

I reach for my Lias necklace—the feel of the raised hearts and the reminder of pure love they represent—is comforting, especially when I'm tense. I sigh and lower my hand once I remember I don't have it on. "It's late. I'm going to bed. Cass and Calder, you know where the towels and extra blankets are if you need them. See you guys in the morning."

Sebastian follows me into our room and shuts the door. His tone is subdued as he approaches me. "She has blown up an apartment before, Talia."

"I understand," I say as I reach for his tie and pull apart the knot for him. The smell of smoke on him brings the horror of the evening back, so I keep my suddenly misty gaze focused on my hands. "But one thing I'm absolutely sure of is that she would never try to hurt me."

"It could've been you, Little Red," he says, folding his warm hands on my wrists. "That scared the ever-loving shit out of me."

"I'm fine, Sebastian."

"Well, I'm not. Not one fucking bit."

Cupping my face, he makes me meet his gaze. "Tomorrow you're coming to the office with me."

I stiffen. "I don't need a constant babysitter."

"What are you talking about?" he says, frowning. "My men are good investigators, but you're the best one I know. Certainly the most tenacious with the details." He releases me and pulls his tie off. "Calder called me out on missing a couple of those tonight."

I frown. "That was shitty. Everyone's emotions were running high."

"He was right." His mouth turns down as he tosses his tie onto the bed. "They were color-related misses. As of tonight, my whole BLACK Security team knows about my color-blindness. I won't risk another issue related to my inability to see color."

"I'm sorry tonight forced you to reveal that." He's such a proud man; that had to have been hard for him to admit to his men, but I'm also relieved. Now they can watch his back too.

"I should've done it before now." Shaking his head, my husband slides his fingers into my hair. "I need them to back me up where I'm not at my best. Just like I need your keen eye on this case to help me sift through the details so we can uncover who's behind this before someone else gets hurt. No more arguing…you're coming."

My heart jumps at his compliment. He's right. I need to help him resolve this quickly. Nodding, I press a kiss below the gauze on his palm. "Take a shower so we can get some sleep. I want to head into the office early."

Resting my hand on his chest for a moment, I start to pull away, but Sebastian's hand folds over mine. I glance down to see him sliding my wedding ring back on my finger. "I don't want it off you for even a day, Little Red. Never take it off again."

"But the wedding—"

He shakes his head. "You're my *wife*."

The tension in his hold twists my heart. As I fold my fingers closed and nod my agreement, he kisses the ring on my finger and heads for the shower.

With the steady patter of the shower in the background, I slide on a thin tank top after washing my face. Isabel's death is devastating and I'm concerned about the danger the rest of the family might be in. I was so relieved Sebastian suggested that Gavin, Damien, Mina and Josi stay with their father for the next few days for better security and all the Blake siblings agreed. I knew it was to support their father, but they're stronger together and they need each other right now. Mina's heartbroken expression flickers through my head. I won't admit to Sebastian that

I'm worried about her, but I plan to stay in closer touch to make sure she's doing okay.

Each time my eyes drift close, the image of the fire billowing out of the limo replays over and over in my head. That could've been Sebastian and me. Worse, it could've been Sebastian. I don't think I could handle being left behind, not now that he's become so important in my life. He's not just my other half, he's the reason I smile every day when I wake up. My eyes pop back open and I shove the upsetting thoughts away, forcing myself to think about the investigation instead.

Sebastian's reminder of my aunt's part in blowing up our apartment bounces around in my head. Could she really hurt me if she felt rejected? Am I wrong in thinking she would never try to inflict physical harm? I shake my head, refusing to go down that dark rabbit hole.

Sebastian lifts the covers and slides into bed behind me. I don't resist when he wraps his arm around my waist and tucks my back against his naked body. Instead, I snuggle closer, appreciating his warmth and the masculine smell of sandalwood soap.

"I'm surprised you're still awake," he murmurs, lifting me so my head rests on his folded bicep.

"My mind is spinning too much."

"Thinking about tomorrow?"

"So many things, but yes, after you told us about Banks's run-in with you earlier today, and the fact he never called me back, it makes me wonder if he ever got my other message through the pizza delivery."

"Even though the asshole didn't deserve your heads up, that was very creative."

"Thanks, but since Banks wasn't arrested, I have to assume the painting wasn't there by the time the police arrived."

"Which means he got your message but chose to believe the worst anyway, hence him confronting me in the street. I'm going to make Stan and Nathan pay for fucking with your safety. I'll—"

"You're going to *stay* out of my business and let me fight my own battles," I say firmly. If he confronts Stan or Nathan, he'll learn that I'm not working there anymore. I'm going to use this time to become an invaluable member of the BLACK Security team. That way maybe whatever hang-ups Sebastian has as to why he hasn't asked me to join him before now hopefully won't matter. "I've taken time off for work for the honeymoon. I don't need to go back for a bit yet, which gives me time to help the investigation. I'll deal with them later."

Sebastian grunts his annoyance, but kisses the side of my neck. "I'm glad you agreed to help."

"Our family was struck hard tonight. I'll do whatever it takes to find the people responsible."

"We'll uncover who's responsible for Isabel's death, but the potential danger to the rest of our family is my priority until the threat is neutralized," he says as he slides his fingers down my arm.

"All lives matter, past and present," I say on a sad sigh.

"You matter the most." The rumble of his words vibrates against my back as his fingers slowly move down my arm, gently massaging my skin along the way.

"It could've been both of us." I close my eyes to hold back the tears at the thought.

The tips of my fingers tingle when he takes extra time on the heel of my hand. My toes twitch with pleasure at the sensation of his thumb pressing along my palm. "The idea that I wouldn't be able to touch you ever again—that it could've been you—ran through my head too many times to count since that bomb went off, Talia."

The pain in his gravelly voice sends a shiver through me just as he rolls my fingers between his. "You're stuck with me, for better or worse," I say in a soft voice. He's lulling me with his magical touch; my body is both relaxed and tingling with each stroke of his fingers.

Sebastian reaches for my chin and tilts my head back to run his fingers along my throat. "No matter how many times I try, my imagination can never recreate the pleasure I get from touching you. Your skin is so soft and I fucking can't get enough of the way you smell."

"Did you know that I bury my face in your pillow every morning before I get up?"

He pauses his massage. "No, I didn't." Sliding his hand

to my collarbone, he presses me to his chest, his erection hard against my rear. "I need to be closer, Little Red."

Sebastian's tension echoes my own. The thought of losing him screamed in my head the whole time he and Calder were gone chasing that car. I didn't let how upset I was show for Mina's sake, but I also didn't exhale deeply until my husband returned. Even now my heart races with worry that the crazy person who did this tonight will try again.

I run my hand along his bare ass and dig my fingers into the tight muscle. Pulling his hips fully against me, I silently agree with his sentiment.

As Sebastian lifts my thigh and slowly eases himself inside me, a couple tears escape, dripping onto his arm.

We don't speak and he doesn't move once he's fully inside me. Flattening his hand on my chest, he says in my ear, "This is peace. No matter what goes on out there, being inside you and feeling your heat surrounding me… you always ground me."

Another tear leaks out. I'm so choked up that my voice croaks a little. "I've never let another person get this close to me. And now, I'm not sure if I'm capable of existing without you." I fold my arm around his under my head, wrapping my fingers around his forearm. "I can never lose you, Sebastian."

"You won't." He kisses my neck, then whispers in my ear, "I'll always be here to protect you."

I shake my head and sniff back the tears, the sensation of his palm and wrist's slight movement making my nipples jut forward for more. "I just want your love."

He slides his hand under my breast and presses his palm against my heart, the act also pushing me to his chest. "Do you feel that, sweet Talia? That's two hearts beating hard despite the fact neither of us is moving." He slides his thumb forward and runs it slowly over my nipple, then stops and leaves it there. "Love, passion, respect. Close your eyes and breathe me in."

I close my eyes and take a deep breath. The sensory overload of the silk sheets and his hard body cocooning me while he's filling me up is so arousing that my breath hitches as I exhale. I love this man so much. I start to speak, but I gasp instead. He's thickening and hardening.

"Do you feel me loving you right now?"

His voice is hoarse, his body so tense, I realize that he's holding back, forcing himself to remain still for me. "I feel you loving me in every move you make," I whisper just before I flex my core muscles tight around him.

He exhales harshly and quickly moves his hand between my thighs. Folding his fingers around me in a tight grip, he nips at my ear, then rasps, "Don't move."

Several seconds tick past where we don't speak. I feel his heart thrumming and that makes mine rev in kind. His hand cupping me in a possessive hold feels so good, I want to move but a part of me doesn't. The intimacy of just feeling his body wrapped around mine from head to toe, his tense hold tightening with each breath we take is a kind of escalating bliss I've never felt before.

Maybe it's the tragic circumstances, or maybe it's our own emotions about the uncertainty of life heightening the moment, but even though my heart is racing and my body is aching for release, I mentally force myself not to move against his hand; I don't want to let what's happening go any more than he does. But when Sebastian clamps his teeth on my shoulder at the same time his tight hold flexes on my sex, I lose complete control as my orgasm takes over my body in hard, gasp-inducing spasms of pleasure.

Releasing my shoulder, Sebastian lets out a primal rumble of satisfaction and buries himself deeper while riding his own climax on the tail end of my euphoria.

That was so beautiful, silently emotional, and incredibly fulfilling, I blink in the darkness, speechless.

Sebastian runs his nose along my temple. "Little Red…"

He sounds contemplative, so I respond in kind. "Mister Black…"

"There are no words." Stunned awe laces his deep voice as he kisses my knuckles.

I bury my fingers in his hair and pull his head close, nodding my agreement.

"I'm staying right here." Nipping at my earlobe, he flattens his palm on my belly and fuses his hips to mine.

"I'm not letting you go," I whisper and close my eyes, extremely thankful that we have each other.

CHAPTER ELEVEN

Talia

"I saw the news last night. I wanted to call, but thought it would be too late. I'm sorry for your loss. Are you okay, Talia?"

"It was tragic and the family is dealing as best as we can, but I'm fine, Nathan." *Why did I answer my cell without looking at the Caller ID?*

"I was shocked by that news, but even more shocked when I came into work this morning and learned that you had resigned. If your husband made you quit after how hard you worked to get back into this business—"

"Stop right there, Nathan. Sebastian had nothing to do with me quitting. It was my choice. Period. End of story."

"But you're a fantastic investigator. I won't let you give that up."

"Who says I'm giving it up?" When I hear Sebastian's voice approaching his office, I say, "I really have to go now, Nathan. I'm okay. Thanks for calling."

I hang up just as Sebastian enters the office with a tall, sandy-haired man in a dark suit and three-day beard scruff. The man looks like he'd been athletic when he was in his twenties, but too many beers and less time in the gym have turned sculpted muscles into less defined bulk in his forties.

"Talia, this is Detective Phil Mayhew. Phil, this is my wife, Talia. She works for the Tribune as an investigator, but is helping us comb through the data in the hopes of capturing the person responsible for yesterday's bombing."

"It's nice to meet you, Talia. Like I was telling Sebastian. Other than Mrs. Blake's body, this folder is all the evidence from the limo worth noting. We interviewed the limo driver, but he only remembers driving away and then nothing else."

Opening the folder, Sebastian frowns, then silently slides one of the photos across his office table to me.

I gasp and snatch up the photo, taking in the mangled, half-melted chain and blackened dual hearts on the locket. "My necklace!" I meet the detective's brown gaze, blinking away the mist in mine. "This was found in the limo?"

He glances Sebastian's way, then nods. "Do you know how your necklace ended up under the floor mat?"

"My wife is *not* a suspect, Phil. Is that clear?"

The detective clears his throat. "The police have their job to do, Sebastian. I'm here as a courtesy, but now that I know the necklace belongs to your wife, I'll have to report my findings to the detectives working the case."

"It's fine, Sebastian. I thought I'd lost my necklace in my old apartment," I tell the detective. "I was there cleaning yesterday and I took the necklace off. I knew I'd need a shower afterward, but the photos in the locket would be ruined if I showered with it on. After my shower, I went to put it on. Unfortunately, I couldn't find my necklace. I looked everywhere for it, but I ran out of time before I had to be home to get dressed for the rehearsal."

Sebastian rests his hands on my shoulders as I stare at the photo with misty eyes. *How did my necklace end up in a burned limo?*

"Didn't you drop your purse on the floor?" Sebastian asks. "Was it in your purse?"

I jerk my gaze to his. "That's it! My purse was the one place I never thought to check for my necklace. It must've been in there the whole time."

Nodding his agreement, he sets the other photo on the table. "This appears to be some sort of small wired bomb with an igniter."

Phil points to the picture. "That's the culprit. According to the reports, they believe it this bomb was attached to the gas tank flap and that's what caused the massive explosion. Based on the size of the bomb, if it had been anywhere else on the vehicle other than near a fuel source, the damage would've been minimal. This was no freak accident."

The photo is of several pieces of warped, blackened metal and a tiny circuit board. It's hard to tell anything from it. "How big was it?" I ask.

"The tech guys said it was no bigger than one by two and a half inches."

"You said the gas tank flap? If it was on the outside of the limo the whole time, someone would've noticed that," I say, tapping my finger on the photo.

Sebastian nods his agreement. "Did the tech guys make a rendering of the device so we can see what it would've looked like? I wonder if we could uncover serial numbers on it."

"I can see if they made a rendering, but unfortunately the device was severely damaged by the fire, so I'm not sure if there would be any serial numbers left on any of the parts. I'm sorry I don't have more, but that's it."

"Could you possibly get us a copy of all the photos taken from the scene?" I ask.

"And leave those," Sebastian says, nodding to the photos. "We'd also like the piece parts of the device and the crime scene investigator's reports."

Phil shakes his head as he sets the empty folder on the table. "You don't ask for much, do you, Sebastian."

"I've consulted for the police department on tons of cases. If they balk at sharing info, tell them to consider this a favor for our help in shutting down that illegal MMA ring a few months ago. That was a big win for your current Chief."

"I'll see what I can do." Phil pauses in the doorway, his hand on the doorknob. "I'm sorry for your family's loss. You know we'll do what we can to bring the culprit to justice."

Sebastian gives him a curt nod, then says in a non-negotiable tone, "We need the rest today, Phil."

"What did you do for him that he's so accommodating?" I ask once the detective shuts the door.

Sebastian slides the two photos back into the folder. "Normally the Blake name is enough. Blake Industries brings in millions to the city, and my father has funded many political campaigns, including the mayor and members of the city council. But I also got Phil out from under a huge gambling debt his eighteen-year-old kid racked up."

"How'd you do that?"

He flashes a dark smile. "Having a tech whiz like Elijah came in very handy for discovering dirt Phil could use as leverage against the loan sharks."

I've met several of Sebastian's team, but never the ever-helpful Elijah. "When am I going to meet Elijah? I swear, I'm beginning to think he's a very real-sounding AI who lives only in the computer system."

"I wish an AI computer had his intuitive hacking skills;

I'd save a mint in Compensation and Benefits. Elijah's not cheap, but he's worth every penny. You'll get to meet him soon enough once he's done pulling every camera feed Calder identifies from the street in front of the church."

"Which is completely legal?" I ask, raising my eyebrows.

"When you swim with sharks, your teeth need to be just as sharp."

I know Sebastian's fighting to protect his family from further threats. Sometimes timely data retrieval is hard to come by, but I prefer getting data the old fashioned way if possible…through contacts. My stomach growls and I glance at my watch. I can't believe it's almost lunchtime already. I planned to check on Mina after I eat. "Have you talked to your father or sister today?"

Sebastian's phone rings and he holds it up, his expression tense as he hits the speaker button. "Hey, Mina. How's Adam holding up?"

"He left for work before the sun rose. Can you believe that crap?" she snaps.

Sebastian sets the phone on the table and leans on it with both hands, tension in his face. "Tell me one of the guys went with him."

"Gavin did. Damien drank until he passed out last night."

"How are you doing?"

"Actually, I'm beyond annoyed at the moment. Can

you believe the restaurant is trying to bill us for being no shows for last night? The manager even tried to deny that Mom had issues with their service right before we were due to arrive." She stops talking and exhales an unsteady breath, her voice rising. "I just don't need that kind of stress. Now that I have the funeral arrangements done, I've got to put together an announcement for the paper."

"Leave the restaurant to me and don't announce anything in the paper, Mina. There's too much risk right now."

She sighs. "Of course. Duh! Sorry, I'm running on autopilot."

"Mina, I'm here too," I say, relieved to hear Mina is in planning mode. "If you need help with Josi so you can run errands and such, we'll be glad to watch her."

"Thank you, both. I may need your help as the time draws closer. Oh, the funeral service is on Wednesday at four. The director asked that the family be there by three-thirty."

"I have to continue to work the investigation, Mina. It's the only way to keep everyone safe, so I won't be attending the funeral."

My gaze snaps to Sebastian. When complete silence comes across the line, my husband lifts his gaze to mine. I shake my head, but I understand why he's chosen not to attend.

"You're joking, right?" Mina's surprised tone shifts to

frustration. "Seb, I know you didn't care that much for my mother, but it's a Blake funeral for God's sake! She's family."

"I'll be doing my part protecting the rest of you," he says in a tense tone as he straightens to slide his hands in his slacks' pockets.

"The family needs you there. *I* need you."

I see the struggle in his expression and I swallow the lump in my throat. I know what's at stake for Sebastian.

"Mina, you know I'd do anything for you. I'm sure you're in pain right now, but this is one request I just can't agree to."

"I can't freaking believe this!" As Mina's voice rises, I stand and move to his side. Sebastian wraps his arm around me and pulls me close as she rants. "We welcomed you into our home, made you a part of our family and this is the thanks we get? *I* get? What am I supposed to say to those attending who ask why you're not there? I don't even want to think what the tabloids will say about this!"

Does Mina realize how much she sounds like her mother at the moment? My stomach churns and I feel so torn by Mina's reaction that I try to smooth over the tense situation. "Mina, our offer still stands to babysit Josi while you're busy with all the arrangements for the funeral. We want to do what we can to support you."

"But not *this*? I'm sorry, Talia, but no thank you. If this is how my supposed *brother* is going to act, he doesn't deserve to spend time with his goddaughter. Not now, not ever."

The line goes dead, but the silence in the room is the worst. I look at Sebastian and the tormented haze in his eyes tears me up inside. I know this is one time my husband cannot compromise, nor should he have to. I touch his jaw and wait until his blue eyes meet mine. "She'll come around, Sebastian. She loves you and Josi adores you. She's just hurting right now."

He folds me in his arms, his expression grim. "I don't know if this will pass, Talia. The whole Blake family will see this as a slap in the face. I sincerely wish that weren't the case, but I can't change it."

"I know you're staying silent for Mina's sake, but what good does it do you if you remain estranged from her because of it? I think you're being a bit too protective of your little sister. She's tough under that sweet exterior. Life is also about experiences and if she doesn't have those—both good and bad—how can she learn to become as strong as she can be?"

"Mina's not the only one I'm protecting." He hooks his hands at the base of my spine. "I'm safeguarding the family name now too, even if I'll no longer be welcome as a part of it."

"That's not right that you're on the right side of this issue, but your honor and loyalty won't be understood or appreciated." I rest my head on his chest and exhale a frustrated sigh.

"Sacrifice is never the easy path. Sometimes it's not the perfect path either, but in my case, it's the only one that honors my mother's memory." He folds his fingers in my hair, pulling the ends to his nose. "I'll survive, Little Red."

Knuckles rap on the door just before Calder walks in, a stack of printouts in hand. "No location on Talia's aunt yet. We think she might've gone away for the weekend. Her house is quiet. Phil sent this paperwork. He said he only got a card from me, so that's the email he used to send this large file. The top one is the rendering of the igniter they found at the—" A ringing cell phone cuts him off and he pulls his phone from his pocket. "What's up, Theo?" Calder frowns and looks at Sebastian. "The entire detail covering the Blake estate has been asked to leave. Did you request this?"

"Fucking hell," my husband mutters. Glancing at the paperwork in Calder's hand, he takes the phone from his cousin. "Pull the men off the grounds, Theo, but don't leave. Stay outside the perimeter of the estate. We'll call you back."

Sebastian hands Calder his phone, then picks up his own cell from the table and dials a number. "Hey, should you be at work? Of course, I'm at the office. Where else would I be?" he grumbles. "Fair point, old man. Question: Do you agree that the family's safety is your number one priority, no matter your feelings on anything else? Good.

Now tell your daughter to allow my men to do their damn jobs."

His father's voice rumbles on the line and my husband glances my way. "I'd planned to have lunch with Talia."

I quickly mouth, "Go, he needs you right now."

"But she's okay to reschedule for tomorrow. I'll be there in twenty minutes."

Hanging up, he looks at Calder. "Can you head over to the family estate and make sure my sister follows orders?"

"Why would Mina not want to be protected?"

Sebastian lifts his suit jacket off the chair and slips into it. Buttoning the front, he says, "She's being difficult. Mina's angry because I told her I'm not going to the funeral."

Calder blinks at his cousin. "Bash, I know you despised Isabel, but even I think that's taking things to the extreme. It's not like you're being asked to give a eulogy."

"I'll be busy working the case to keep the family safe."

"What kind of bullshi—"

"I'm going to be late if I don't leave now to meet my father," Sebastian says. He glances my way and I wave him on.

"Why are you still here? I'll look over the rendering and see if we can magnify the other picture to read possible serial numbers."

Stepping close, Sebastian kisses my forehead and says in a low voice, "Did you know you were going to lose the bet?"

His question throws me for a second, then I remember that I'd mentioned cleaning the apartment to the detective. I give him a secret smile to cover my blunder. "Now that we're giving up the lease on the apartment, maybe your office can become my new home away from home."

"You're already an invaluable member of our team."

"But I haven't done anything yet."

"I didn't say what team I was talking about."

"Get a room, you two," Calder snorts.

Snickering, I smile at my husband. "Go enjoy lunch with your father."

The moment Sebastian leaves, Calder turns to me, his amusement gone. "What the hell is going on with Sebastian? This funeral thing seems extreme."

"Do you trust him, Calder?"

His light brown brows pull together. "Of course. More than anyone."

"Trust me when I say that Sebastian's only goal is to protect his family."

"To the point of aliening himself?"

"I believe you did something similar not that long ago. I'm going to assume you had your reasons?" When his only answer is to press his lips together, I raise my eyebrow. "Was Sebastian there for you?"

He stares at me for a second, then tilts his head, his green eyes drilling into me. "Yeah, he was." With a curt nod, he hands me the stack of papers and starts to leave, but turns back. "Thanks, Talia."

"For what?"

"Reminding me what being a brother means."

I smile, relieved that Calder will have Sebastian's back. "You're welcome."

My phone rings as he walks out. I glance down at the Caller ID this time and know I can't ignore this one.

"Hey, Aunt Vanessa."

"Talia! I just found out what happened at your wedding rehearsal. I'd gone to stay at a Bed and Breakfast for a couple of days and didn't see the news until this morning. I'm so sorry, dear, but also so very glad you're safe."

My aunt's voice is so shaky, I feel horrible for not inviting her to the wedding sooner. "I'm fine. Of course the family is mourning Isabel's death, so the wedding has been pushed back for the funeral and while an investigation is going on. Also, since I have you, I wanted to let you know you'll be getting your invitation with the new date of the wedding in the mail soon."

"Oh, Talia…that makes me so happy. Thank you! I wouldn't miss it! Of course now I'm worried about what happened. Please tell me it was an accident and that you're not in any danger."

"I'm fine, Aunt Van—" My heart jolts as my gaze lands on the top page of the stack of papers Calder gave me. I stare at the rendering of the igniter from the police's tech department. *Oh, shit!*

"Talia? Is everything okay?"

"Yes, I'm good, but I really have to go now. We have a lot to do."

I hang up and stare at the drawing. It looks exactly like the "tracker" I chucked into the water fountain outside the Fine Tapas restaurant.

I'm pretty sure the water would've compromised the circuitry, rendering its igniter component useless against the bit of explosive compound, but if I can retrieve it we might be able to get serial numbers off that one. All I can hope is that it's actually not a GPS tracker like I thought, and if it's still sending a signal that the person who planted it on my car hasn't found it yet.

I quickly grab my purse and walk out into the cubicle area, then remember I rode to the office with Sebastian. Frustrated, I glance around the couple of occupied desks and know that the men are busy working aspects of the case for Sebastian. Calder just left to deal with Mina and the last thing I'll do is pull Sebastian away from much needed quality time with his father. Biting my lip, I retrieve my phone and dial the only other person I can trust to give me a ride.

CHAPTER TWELVE

Sebastian

"Hey," I say as my half-brother, Gavin, walks out of Adam's outer office door.

He just sneers and brushes past me.

"That bad, huh?"

"What do you care?" He turns and buttons his suit jacket, his hazel green eyes drilling into me. "You're ditching your family on a day when tragedy should unite us, and yet *he's* choosing you over me."

Mina must've told Gavin I'm not attending the funeral. Guess I'm back on the black list. It always was my best color. "It's just lunch, Gavin."

He stiffens. "It's never just lunch with him. As for your wedding, whatever day it gets rescheduled, I've got to work."

My hand curls tight around my car keys in my pocket. "That hurts Talia. She doesn't deserve that."

"You didn't think twice about hurting Mina. I don't know if you thrive on burning relationships to the ground or what, but if you fuck with our father the way you just did our sister, I'll cut you off at the knees."

Narrowing my gaze on him, I turn and walk into the office, shutting the door. If I don't, I'll put my fist through his face.

Adam's on the phone when I enter his office. He nods to acknowledge my presence and gestures for me to sit in the leather chair in front of his desk.

He's talking in a fast clip, negotiating the terms of a development agreement. As I stare at his graying dark hair, it occurs to me that Talia's right. I do look like my father. I'm seeing a version of myself thirty years in the future. Except I wouldn't be this calm if I'd just lost Talia. I'd be out there wreaking havoc and breaking any laws necessary to ferret out the bastard who took my wife from me. He would pay in the most painful way possible.

But my father and I definitely both use work to keep us sane. Considering my personal feelings for Isabel, I decide it's best to keep the subject on business. The moment he hangs up, I lift my chin toward the paperwork he's putting away. "Sounds like you got what you wanted."

"I'm not in a mood to be messed with."

My eyebrow hikes. "Is that a warning for how this

meeting is going to go?"

Adam Blake's expression remains serious as he comes around to rest his thigh on his desk in front of me. "I can't imagine anyone intentionally wanting to harm us. What did your police contact say caused the explosion?"

"Unfortunately it was intentional. Someone planted a bomb on the limo. The only way something that small could've caused the explosion the way it did was if it was put right on the gas tank flap."

My father's eyes mist over and he glances away, clearing his throat. "Do they have any leads?"

"None that I'm aware of yet, but we're also working the case. I'll let you know as soon as something develops."

"Definitely keep me in the loop. While you were on your way over here, Den asked to schedule a meeting after ours. He wants me to meet an old MI6 colleague of his who's here in town. He's considering moving to New York."

"If he's looking for a job, it's probably a good idea to expand your security team, especially if the man is anywhere close to Den's caliber."

"If Den recommends him, I'll definitely meet him, but now that it's just me..." Adam shrugs. "One guard is enough. But if I feel good about him, I might send the man your way. Are you looking to expand your team some more?"

"Our team has worked, because I've hand picked the

men based on working together on past jobs."

"Understood. I'll only let you know if he impresses the hell out of me." Adam runs his hand down his tie. "Since I have that meeting right be hind this, are you okay to eat here? Ms. Shaw has ordered sandwiches for us."

"Are you going to admit that you can't work through all your grief? You should take some time off."

"You mean like you're taking some time off by not attending the funeral?"

When I open my mouth to speak, he sighs and shakes his head. "I'm still coming down from my aggressive negotiator mode. I don't expect you to be there, Sebastian."

I'm so stunned, I can't respond for a couple seconds. "You don't?"

"No, I truly don't." Adam folds his hands together, resting them on his thigh. "I know Isabel wasn't the kindest to you when you first came to live with us, and that's on me that I didn't correct her attitude years ago." I start to speak, but he shakes his head. "I can't take that past back, but I can respect your decision about the funeral."

I rest my right ankle over my knee and dip my head, appreciating his understanding. "Are you going to tell me what this meeting is about?"

"Right." Adam stands, then moves around to sit behind his desk.

Ms. Shaw, an older woman who guards him like a dragon, knocks and walks in with two white bags, handing each of us one. "Your lunch is a chicken sandwich on freshly made buns and kettle chips from The Bistro."

My father unwraps his sandwich from the white waxy paper and takes a bite. Rumbling his approval, he grabs a folder and slides it across the desk toward me.

"What's this?" I swallow the bite of soft hoagie bread and open the folder. A couple seconds later, I jerk my gaze to his.

"I want you to take some time to think about it, Sebastian."

I glance back down at the succession plan he's outlined. It shows me taking over as President and CEO of Blake Industries when he retires in three years time. Gavin is listed as Senior Vice President and Chief Operating Officer, and Damien is listed as Senior Vice President and head of Sales and Business Development. All four of the Blake siblings will have equal shares in the company.

Adam's expression is hopeful. "Damien is happiest in a role where he can get out there and schmooze. Mina has mentioned wanting to go back to work once Josi is ready for preschool. When she's ready to come back she'll work in tandem with the marketing director and move up as she learns the business. She has a great eye for ways to expand our social media presence and other ad opportunities. I'd like you to start working with me as soon as possible consulting on projects for now, Sebastian. Then you can transition over time."

I close the folder and set it back on his desk, then take another bite of the chicken. I chew slowly, then finally speak. "It looks like you've got it all worked out, but as I've told you, I have my own business to run."

Adam steeples his fingers and tilts his head. "I think BLACK Security would make a fantastic addition to the company's portfolio. We need to beef up our own internal security anyway. It's way overdue. You'll get top dollar for your company. That's how much I want you in this role, Sebastian."

"Why me?" I rub my chin and hold his gaze. "Gavin has worked with the company since he graduated college. He has always assumed he would succeed you. Why change the players?"

My father's blue gaze sharpens. "You think I didn't know you were behind the purchase of our Hamptons home? I knew, Sebastian. I also know what's going on with your company. I've kept tabs on you since you left the Navy. I watched you start your business from nothing, and not only did you make it work, but you expanded it and managed to significantly increase your bottom line. Very impressive."

He picks his sandwich back up but doesn't take a bite of the hoagie. "Your employees' loyalty is the best I've ever seen. Yes, I'm sure some of that has to do with serving together, but there's so much more to leading people than just having past ties. Being a good leader can't be learned.

It's ingrained. You have all the qualities I want in a CEO for Blake Industries. I'm damned lucky you also happen to be my son."

It hits me why he's doing this now. My father knew Isabel would flip out if he made this announcement while she was alive. The document in that folder was drafted by his finance and legal teams months ago, yet he didn't tell anyone. Until now. Isabel's death didn't cause him to decide on this, but it definitely accelerated his plan to disclose it now.

"You need to give Gavin a chance to prove himself." When my father frowns at my suggestion, I hold my hand up. "For all you know, Gavin's been reining in his leadership skills because you were at the helm. I recommend that you start including him in more top-level aspects of the business. Promote him to Chief Operating Officer now. Not only will he feel recognized for the contributions he has made to the company, but the new job will also expose him to how you run a business on all levels. You might be surprised at his ideas if you give him a role with the authority to affect changes he thinks will benefit the company. If you do it while you're still around and very active in day-to-day business, you can guide him and help make sure his decisions are in the company's overall best interest for the short and long term."

"Are you saying you don't want to be part of Blake Industries?"

I know my answer matters to Adam for reasons he'll never share. "I'm saying that Gavin deserves a shot at it. If he flounders, I'll be there to help, but he needs a chance to prove he can be just as successful if not more so than you were."

"And BLACK Security?"

"Remains mine," I say, finishing the last bit of my sandwich. "But if you need my help in any aspect of your business, from background checks, to security breeches either financial or IT related, to extra security for an event or a special guest you're hosting, you only have to ask."

"You just outlined a contract with BLACK Security I could get my head around," my father says, a brief smile curving his lips. "Get me a write up and we'll talk numbers."

I'm not sure how I feel about working with my father, but he wants me here, then it may as well be on my terms. "Sounds like a plan."

The room grows quiet and Adam's mood turns somber. "She had her frustrating moments, but I miss Isabel."

"I'm truly sorry for your loss."

Adam nods his appreciation, then looks contemplative. "How's Talia doing with the wedding being postponed?"

"You know Talia…right now she's helping me with the investigation."

"Hold on tight to that woman, son. She's the quiet storm our family needs."

"Quiet storm?"

He nods. "Quiet storms enter on a whisper. They're not harsh or violent, but their winds can be powerfully strong, turning the biggest of boats around and putting them back on course."

I smile at his accurate assessment. Talia really won over Adam. I wish I could've overheard their conversation about me. A text comes through from Calder just as I nod my agreement with my father.

Waiting for you outside. Thanks to Talia we have a serial number to run down.

I look at my father, but don't want to share the development in case it doesn't pan out. "Thanks for lunch and the discussion."

We stand together and my father puts out his hand. "I'm looking forward to working with you, son."

I clasp his hand and shake it, nodding. "I'll work up the contract and get you a copy to review."

"What's the serial number from? That igniter was toast," I say to Calder as I approach.

"But the other one wasn't." He pushes off from leaning against my car and uncurls his hand, revealing a device that looks just like the rendering I glanced at before we left.

"What other one?" My stomach tenses. *How did Talia get a hold of another device?*

Calder lifts up his phone and Talia's voice comes through the speaker. "Remember when I fussed at you and said, "Even in redundancy mode?"

My body tenses and I grab the device from Calder's hand. "You meant that *literally*?" I pull open the igniter's casing and look for the serial number, while my brain seizes on the fact that it was on her car.

"Knowing your need to have a backup plan, I found the second device that I thought *you* had put there and tossed it into a water fountain outside the restaurant."

"How did you retrieve this from the fountain?" I instantly frown, then grate out, "Did you leave the office by yourself?"

"Well, I had to—"

"Never mind." The tightness in my chest grows tighter. "Where are you right now?"

"At the office."

"I'll be right there."

"Calm down, Bash. Den is with her," Calder says.

"No, he's not," I snap. "He's meeting with my father right now."

"Actually, my MI6 colleague is interviewing with Adam as we speak," Den's British accent floats from Calder's speaker phone. "Due to the high threat level on Talia, I just informed your father before I called you that I'm taking over as her personal bodyguard, effective immediately."

I'm both relieved and pissed. "You're not a member of

my team."

"Then fix that, Mr. Blake," Den says in a formal tone.

I look at Calder, my expression saying, *Can you believe the balls on this guy?* "Mr. Blake is my father," I say curtly, frustrated that I'm not already by my wife's side.

"Then fix that, *sir*."

Calder smirks and I shake my head. "Sebastian will do."

"Talia is my priority," Den says. "Her car has been dusted for prints and there weren't any others than hers. Go find the bastard who's trying to hurt her."

"We'll discuss salary *and* boundaries later."

"Boundaries mean nothing. Only people matter."

I blink at the dead line. *That fucker hung up on me.*

"Congratulations, looks like he's decided to hire you as his boss." Calder chuckles as he puts his phone away and walks around to stand beside the passenger door.

"Did you know about this?" My hand tightens around my keys.

He shrugs. "You know that Den's presence is the only way you'll go with me to follow this lead."

I don't like the idea of not going straight back to the office. Talia fully trusts Den and if I can't be there personally, his extensive skill set is exactly the kind of guard I want watching my wife's back.

Beeping the car to unlock it, I open my door and grumble, "Get in. It's getting late."

We drive for a while, then enter a sketchier area of the Lower East Side. "Keep on this road and we'll be there in less than ten minutes," Calder says

"Good thing we left when we did." I glance at my watch. "The store you say the electronic part came from will close soon. Other than convenience stores, no one in this area sticks around late if they don't have to, and I'm sure Vinny's Electronics won't be any different."

Rolling his head from one shoulder to the other, Calder glances my way. "Even when I was going through all my shit and I'd stayed away from family for months, I still managed to make it to Josi's christening. You know I support you regardless, but what could possibly be so bad that would make you risk alienating everyone else?"

I thrum my fingers on the dashboard, knowing that Calder won't let this go. In about five seconds he'll say something else. *Five, four, three, two—*

"Seriously, Bash. You're my brother! Fucking talk to—"

"Isabel paid a hit man to take me out when I was a teen," I snap. "My mom was his victim instead."

"Holy shit!" Calder shoves his hands through his hair and stares for a beat. "That's so fucked up, I can't even wrap my head around it. There's no way you've known about this the whole time or sneering at Isabel is the least you would've done to her."

I nod. "The man Isabel hired back then was that Hayes guy from Talia's past. The day Hayes attacked Talia in her apartment, he told me how Isabel hired him all those years ago. It's a good thing he tried to kill me again after that sick confession, because that bastard was going down either way. How's that for twisted fuckery?"

Calder folds his arms, angry lines bracketing his mouth. "Isabel deserved jail, not a memorial honoring her memory. Why didn't you say anythi—"

"You can't repeat *any* of this." I stop for a car waiting to turn left in front of me and meet his gaze, my expression resolute. "It would devastate our family."

"You don't deserve the shit you'll get for this," he mutters, then looks down the street as I push on the gas. "The store's sign is up ahead."

"Adam accepts my decision. The others..." I shrug "I guess I'm not surprised. Once a bastard, always a bastard."

He starts to say something, but I pull in front of Vinny's Electronics. Cutting the engine, I peer through Calder's window at the storefront. The Open sign is turned off, but lights are still on in the store.

The store's door doesn't give when I push on it. Instead the lights inside go completely out. "Well, shit."

Calder folds his hand tight around the igniter. "Damn. Looks like we're coming back."

I hear an approaching car slowing down behind us and having seen enough drive-bys in my youth, I instantly reach for Calder's arm, my voice low. "Down, Cald!"

"What?" As Calder ducks slightly and follows my

line of sight, the car revs and zooms away. I stare after it, narrowing my gaze at the car's familiar shape and the shadow of a bob hairstyle on the driver.

I straighten and grumble, "I didn't get to see if it had a unicorn hood ornament."

"You think it's the same car that cut us off?" Calder asks, standing to his full height.

"I might not be able to see the color of the paint, but it's bright and the same body style. I don't believe in coincidences."

"It's a pale yellow."

I try to use the dim taillights to make out the license plate, but the car is too far away and the street too poorly lit. I lift my gaze to the rundown building with a fancy marquee off in the distance. "My old neighborhood isn't far from that old theater. Most likely Banks runs this commercial section too. We'll be back first thing in the morning."

CHAPTER THIRTEEN

Talia

I'm anxious when Sebastian and I wake up. I'm not concerned for myself. I've never felt safer. Den's decision to become my guard shocked me, but I didn't question it. Instead, I felt honored. I respect him and trust his instincts. Even though I fell asleep early, I didn't sleep well since Sebastian told me he was going back to that store in the morning. Of course the store is close to his old neighborhood. *Is Banks behind all this?* Talking about it will only make me more tense, so I decide to focus on other things.

"I crashed before you could tell me about your meeting with your father," I call from the closet once the shower shuts off, then button my lightweight linen jacket over a white blouse. Running my hands over the matching pants,

I start to step into my favorite pair of heels when Sebastian pops into the closet with nothing but a towel around his waist.

I don't even get a chance to admire his gorgeous abs before he wraps his arms around my waist and pulls me close. "I know, sleepyhead. You conked out the moment I pulled you against me."

I grimace. "I'm sorry. How'd it go?"

"I used the quiet time to read through the file from Phil and get caught up to where you were on the details of the case. You have no idea how relieved and proud I am that you checked the other wheel wells and found that device."

"If I didn't have a thorough husband, I might not have."

"So relieved," he repeats softly before he releases me to step out of the towel. While he pulls on a pair of dress pants over his boxers, he says casually, "My father asked me to sell him my business."

"You're not going to, right?" I say, my eyes widening. Sebastian worked hard to establish his BLACK Security company. After listening to him tell me about his business in the office yesterday morning and then walking around and asking questions on my own while I waited for him to return, I thought of so many ways to expand it if he wanted to.

He shakes his head and pulls a dress shirt off the hanger. "I turned him down, but I offered to consult if he needs anything in the future. He countered by asking to set up a contract with me."

"Are you going to?" I watch him button his shirt, my voice full of hope that they'll finally get to really know each other.

Sebastian picks up a couple of ties and turns to me. "Which one?"

He's not wearing the special shirt I gave him. This one is a medium blue and it'll go well with his gray suit, but he's holding the wrong color ties for it. I return them to their slots in his drawer and find a pale yellow one with blue flecks that'll match his shirt and hand it to him. "Try this one."

"Thanks, Little Red." Smiling, he walks into the bathroom to knot his tie in front of the mirror.

I smile after him once I realize this is the second day in a row he asked me which tie. Actually, yesterday he sought out my opinion on his suit too. "Well?"

"He asked me to be CEO. I turned him down, so this is the least I can do to be indirectly involved with his company."

"Adam asked you to run the business?" I follow him into the bathroom and meet his gaze in the mirror, eyes wide. *That's huge.*

He smirks as he folds his shirt collar down over his tie. "Yeah, I wasn't expecting that, but the paperwork he showed me with his succession plan was dated months ago. I told him he needs to let Gavin have a shot at it, but I would be there if needed."

"Then the contract idea is a good way to bridge your involvement. I was looking over what BLACK Security does and as broad as your team's skill sets are today, I think there's so much potential for other areas of growth. Depending on how extensive you make the contract with your father, you could potentially be included in a lot of meetings if you wanted to be."

He smiles his approval at me in the reflection as he smooths his tie and buttons his jacket. "Like I said, you're already a valuable team member."

"You said that comment was about us," I say, giving him a look.

He turns to me, a devilish smile curving his lips. "Did I?" Clasping my face, he lowers his to mine, our lips almost touching. "Why, Little Red, don't you know that statement applied across the board?"

Before I can think of a witty reply, he steals another kiss, this one lingering and so sensual, I sigh as he lifts his head. "Calder's waiting downstairs for me. I've let Den in already. Do not take a breath without him there to hear it."

Laughing, I shake my head. "I'm so glad you're not serious."

I jump when he lands a solid smack on my ass, then hauls me against his hips. "Who says I'm not? At all times, Talia."

Saluting him, I tap his chest just before he moves away. "Don't do anything crazy today. Just get the evidence you need to nail whoever's responsible and let the police handle it."

I walk back into our closet to put my heels on, then sigh that he'd left his towel on the marble-top island in the middle of our closet. I lift the towel up and a small white rectangle label flutters to the floor.

I pick it up and as I return the towel to the bathroom, I realize it's one of the labels Teresa adds to his shirts as part of his color-coding system. Crap, which shirt is missing the tag? I return to our closet and start at the end of his row of shirts, lifting the tail to look for one that's missing the tag. The first one I check must've been it; it's missing its label. But when I look at the label, it doesn't match the shirt. Frowning, I move on to the next shirt, then the next. Several of them are missing their labels. Why are they suddenly falling off? Did she change the adhesive she uses to iron it on?

I open his drawer to put the label inside for safekeeping and pause at the stack of labels neatly set in the corner, exactly how Sebastian would intentionally organize them.

I lift the stack and as I sift through them, big fat tears well. He'd pulled them all off. Every single one. "Oh, Sebastian…"

Returning the labels where I found them, I walk into our bedroom and grab my cell, typing him a message.

Thank you for letting me be your rainbow.

His reply is immediate.

You have always been so.

I smile at his reply. The more I think about what a good man my husband is, the more determined I become with my plan for the day. Stepping into our living room, I pause at the sight of Den sitting by the window drinking a cup of coffee and smile. I especially love that he'd pulled a kitchen chair up close. *A kindred spirit.* "Do you do that when it rains or snows too?"

He clears his throat and immediately stands. "I find it helpful for thinking."

"It's best if you fully face the glass, you know."

"Not when I'm on duty." Walking over to the sink, he rinses his cup, then returns to pick up his gun and slide it into its discrete holster under his arm before he buttons his suit jacket. "Where are we going this morning?"

"I've got a couple of errands to run. First stop…a spa."

When his eyebrows lift, I laugh. "I'm not planning a mani-pedi. This is a data retrieval mission. Fingers crossed, I'll be able to get what I'm looking for."

The Blake estate is quiet as the house manager with silent footsteps, escorts me into the dining room where Mina and Josi are having breakfast.

"Come in, Talia. Would you like some coffee or a croissant with jam?" Mina says as she pulls a pastry apart for Josi, then sets the bits on her highchair tray.

"Where are your brothers and dad?" I ask as I move into the room and take a seat at the table on the other side of Josi's chair.

"They're all at the office today," she says, her blonde hair swaying as she pulls more bread apart for Josi. "Thankfully Damian finally dragged himself out of bed this morning."

"How are you doing?" I ask and smile at Josi when she waves and calls out, "Ahhya, oon, oon!"

"You want a spoon?" Mina says, handing her daughter one.

Josi grabs the utensil and bangs it on her tray a couple of times before throwing it on the carpet.

I laugh and pick it up, setting it on the table. "She's talking about the book, *Goodnight Moon* that I read her the other night." Glancing Den's way, I say, "Could you please close the door, Den?"

Nodding, he pulls the double French doors closed, leaving Mina, Josi, and me alone in the dining room.

"This seems serious," Mina says, her smile melting away.

"You know why I'm here."

Lifting her chin a notch, she sniffs. "Sebastian's at fault here, not me. It's as if he could care less that she died."

"That's not true. He knows you're in pain."

Her brown eyes water, tears threatening. "Then he

should be there. He sacrifices nothing by attending except his time and his pride."

I shake my head and turn in my seat to fully face her. "That's where you're wrong, Mina. You think he's dishonoring your mother—"

"Yes, he is!" she says, cutting me off.

"But what you don't know is that by attending Isabel's funeral, he would be dishonoring his own mother's memory."

She snorts and folds her arms on the table. "Since when is Sebastian so sentimental? Everyone knows my mom never tried to replace his mother. He's being ridiculous. And the rest of the family sees it that way too."

"You told your brothers and dad?"

"Of course I did. They needed to know he wasn't attending."

"Then it's your job to undo the damage," I say, my tone hardening. "The guys were just starting to get along."

Mina frowns, her hands folding tight around her arms. "Why would I do that?"

"He's your brother too."

She rolls her eyes. "No true *Blake* turns their back on family."

I press my lips together to keep from saying something in the heat of anger. This whole thing has really thrown Mina, making her revert back to that immature girl I first met years ago. "I know losing your mom has been awful and hard. I had hoped that instead of being angry with Sebastian about the funeral that you would remember how your brother was there for you when Josi was born, but since you seem determined to hold a grudge, and have now passed your sentiments on to your brothers who already resent Sebastian, you need to know the truth."

When Mina shrugs and looks away as if she couldn't care less, I snap at her, "Look at me, Mina. This is important!"

Huffing, she turns back and adopts a haughty tone. "You have five minutes."

"That's all I'll need." It's hard not to take a defensive tone with her, but I manage to keep mine even and calm. "Sebastian has already sacrificed on a deeply personal level for you, and I won't stand by and let you continue to lash out at him because you don't have all the facts. *You* are the only reason he didn't tell his father the truth and seek full justice for his mother."

"What are you *talking* about?" Mina says, her tone sharpening.

"I would explain it, but I don't think you would believe me, so I'm going to show you." I queue up the video clip that I retrieved from the spa. Sebastian told me about his visit to the spa Isabel frequented where he confronted her about her part in his mother's death and the attempt on his life. I wondered if there might be a recording of their conversation. Sure enough the spa had put cameras in the rooms at discrete angles to protect themselves from potential lawsuits. It took longer than I expected, because my husband had them erase the original tape from their system, expecting the off-site backup to be erased at the same time. He didn't know that the back-up sweep only happened once a quarter. Thankfully the spa bent over backward to please the new owner's wife and discretely retrieved a copy for me before the sweep erased that copy too.

Handing Mina my phone, I say, "Please move away to watch that. I don't want Josi hearing any of it."

She frowns, but moves to the head of the table to watch. My heart aches that I have to share Isabel at her nastiest with her daughter, but I refuse to protect someone's reputation who never deserved it. I'd rather fight for my husband's happiness with his family.

Mina gasps, a shaky hand flying to her mouth as she watches the truth unfold. When her tears spill over, I get up and move to sit in the chair beside her. The moment I'm seated, she lets go of my phone, dropping it on the table as if she can't stand touching it. "I'm sorry, Mina. Sebastian has no idea I'm here, but I love him too much to let his protective silence tear your relationship apart. He deserves better."

Angry eyes cut to me, her voice quavering. "How could you destroy my memory of my mother like that?"

"You'd rather go on believing your brother is a cold-hearted, selfish person who doesn't care about you instead?" Shaking my head, I sigh. "I did what I thought was best for the future of this family as a whole, Mina. If it makes you feel better to blame someone, then blame me, but now it's your turn to be the bigger person and support Sebastian. If you can't see past your hurt to acknowledge his and find a way in your heart to understand—even in your darkest moments—then you were never a true sister to him. Not like the many ways he's been a brother to you."

Picking up my phone, I stand and drop a kiss on Josi's sweet curls on my way out.

CHAPTER FOURTEEN

Sebastian

"Is there a reason you're just now putting your gun on?" Calder says once I cut the car engine, then tuck the compact holster behind my back to keep it hidden.

"I didn't want to upset Talia. If she saw the gun, she'd definitely worry." I nod toward the store. "Elijah said the owner's name is Vincent Karras. On a first pass, his business seems to be legit."

Calder opens his door. "Let's find out."

The store is cramped with various types of electronics and casings. It's a hodge-podge of old and new parts, but somehow the man with curly gray hair sipping coffee at the counter has the parts and bits completely organized in trays and bins on the shelves in the small store.

"Good morning early risers. I'm Vinny. Let me know if

you need my help," he calls from his seat on an old-style metal stool.

I hone in on the small electronics section and walk over to stare at a box of casings like the one used to hold the circuit board and explosive compound inside the igniter. Looking up, I address the owner. "We'd like to know more about these."

His stool scrapes the floor as he stands and walks over to us. "What would you like to know?"

I uncurl my fist and show him the device Talia found on her car. "We traced the path this batch of casings took from the manufacturer to their distributor, and then to your store."

He gives me a wary look as he points to the box with only two casings left. "I have some extra in the back if you need them."

I shake my head and pull the casing off the igniter to show him the serial number. "I just want to know who you sold this particular part to."

He walks away, saying over his shoulder, "Eh, I'm not in the habit of giving out customer information. It's bad for business."

Calder walks over to the door and stands there while I follow the guy back to his small desk next to the wall.

The moment he steps behind the desk and I see his hands shaking, I'm right there standing across from him as he turns around. I set the device on his desk. "The person who built this used another one just like it to kill a family member." Before he can refuse my request, I retrieve my gun from its holster and glance Calder's way as I check the clip, then slide it back into place. "Family is pretty important, wouldn't you say?"

He keeps a stoic expression and slowly nods.

Vinny clears his throat and zips his jacket all way up before quickly tapping on his computer keyboard. "Um, let me see if I can track that down for you."

After I give him the number, he scans through a few screens, nervously glancing my way. "I'm sorry but the few people who purchased that part paid cash, so it's not on record."

He's sweating and it's air-conditioned in his shop.

I turn his screen too fast for him to stop me.

"Hey!" Vinny tries to pull the screen back, but I refuse to let go as I quickly scan for the part. Only one purchase this year, but it definitely stands out.

BB Discount, FREE.

"Which one of his crew bought it?" I bark.

"Banks," he says, eyes wide.

I narrow my gaze, my jaw muscle tensing. "If you warn them I'm coming, I'll be back."

At his fast nod, I return my gun to its holder and nod to Calder. "Let's go."

The moment we pull into my old neighborhood, my phone rings, Mina's number popping up on my Caller ID.

I answer on the first ring. "Is everything all right?"

"Everything is fine. I just wanted you to know that I've thought about what you said and I understand, Seb."

"Mina—"

"It's okay, I really do understand. Also, I've been overwhelmed with taking care of Josi while trying to coordinate everything for the funeral, so if you and Talia are still willing to watch her the night before the funeral and keep her until after it's over, I would appreciate it so much."

"We'll be happy to do that for you. Can I call you back later?"

"Sure, no problem. We can talk later. Thanks, big brother. I owe you."

When she hangs up, I look at Calder, my brows pulling together. "That was...unexpected."

He shrugs. "None of us understand the road trip to forgiveness in a woman's mind. Count your blessings yours was fairly short."

Shaking my head at his answer, I turn onto Banks's road and drive past his house to see how many of his guys might be home. When we round the corner to another street, Paulo leaves the house, whistling and tossing his car keys in the air. The engine of his suped-up muscle car rumbles to life just as I park on another street that'll allow me access to the back side of their home.

We wait another twenty minutes, watching the house,

before I grab my lock-picking kit, stun gun and supplies from the glove compartment. Calder goes around the front and rings the bell while I head to the back.

No one's in the kitchen when I let myself in. Just as I tuck the kit away, a guy steps into the kitchen. He doesn't even get a yelp out before I stun him, then quickly use plastic ties to bind his hands and feet. A cloth gag from the kitchen keeps him quiet.

Male voices rumble in the living room, and as I soundlessly make my way down the narrow hallway, I pause and stare at a picture. Pulling the frame off the wall, I hear Banks bellow in annoyance, "Why does Blackie keep sending people to talk for him?"

A young guy around fifteen, with spiked black hair and tattoos all over his neck, reaches the bottom of the stairs in the hallway when he sees me. I hold up the stun gun and say in a low, intimidating voice, "Go back upstairs and pretend you never saw me or be stunned and hog-tied. Your choice. Don't warn him either."

The punk-looking kid shakes his head and says, "Not my circus," then turns and silently heads back up the stairs.

"It's because the Blackie bastard's too afraid to show up," a short guy with buzzed hair says while standing beside Banks in a show of support of his leader.

"Sebastian wants a neutral meeting place." Calder doesn't let his gaze stray to me as I trade the stun gun for my lethal one and enter the room from the hallway.

Other than the guy standing next to Banks, two guys are in the room sitting on the couch with gaming joysticks in their hands.

"Too fucking bad," Banks snarks at Calder. "If he wants a piece of me, he knows where to find me."

"Yes, I do," I say, right before I toss the picture in his direction.

When Banks captures the frame mid-air, I point my gun at his guys, who'd quickly jumped up from the couch the moment they heard my voice behind them. "I wouldn't if I were you."

"Calm down." Holding the picture, Banks lifts his other hand toward his guys, letting them know not to make any aggressive moves. "What the hell are you doing invading my home?"

I nod to the picture he caught. "You're going to pay for killing a Blake, Banks." I shift my gaze to my cousin. "Does she look familiar?"

When Calder glances down at the image of Banks and the unicorn girl kissing in the photo, he quickly steps back and pulls his own gun. Training it on Banks, he speaks to the guys in his crew, "Stay put. Banks is the only one we're interested in."

"Did I mention my cousin's a SEAL too?" I meet Banks's defiant stare with a cold one. "You just fucked with the wrong family."

CHAPTER FIFTEEN

Talia

O*nce* we pull away from the Blake Estate, my hands start to shake. The tense meeting with Mina got to me and I immediately reach up to touch my necklace. Sighing my frustration and sadness that it's gone, I let my hand drop to my lap.

"To the office?" When I don't immediately reply, Den slides his gaze to me. "Are you all right?"

The downside of refusing to ride in the back is that he can see everything. I offer a rueful half-smile and fold my hands together. "I tried to smooth some ruffled feathers, but I may have just made things irrevocably worse."

He returns his focus to the road, flipping the sun visor down against the bright sun. "You were right to defend him. Isabel wasn't always the nicest person. I don't know what this is all about, but I know Sebastian doesn't do anything without cause. I've seen how much he does for Mina. She's a bit oblivious to that, I think."

I glance his way, surprised he has paid so much attention. "I hope you're right, Den. I have a tendency to go with my gut on things."

"All will be well, Talia."

The confidence in his tone makes me feel a little less stressed. Needing something to distract me, I open my satchel and pull out the paperwork from the bombing that Sebastian read over last night after I zoned out. If I scan over it once more, I can feel confident that we didn't miss anything. The detective, Phil's number is scrawled across the top. Pulling out my phone, I dial it.

"Hi, Mr. Mayhew, this is Talia Blake, Sebastian's wife. Do you know when I'll be able to get my necklace from the police?"

"It's an on-going investigation, Mrs. Blake, but as a favor to the family I'll see what I can do to get it for you. I have a contact in the evidence room."

"Thank you. I really appreciate it."

"Sure, no problem."

"Have you heard of any new leads in the case?"

"None so far. I'll let you know."

It's on the tip of my tongue to share that BLACK Security is already running down a lead, but until I find out more, there's no point. "Well, hopefully the officers will find something soon."

"Yeah, just have to keep working it. I'll be in touch about your necklace."

"Thank you."

Hanging up, I sigh and spend the next ten minutes flipping through the paperwork of reports until I reach the tech person's write up that said since no other accelerant was found, the igniter had to have been located on the gas tank flap to cause the kind of explosion it did. "This is the third time that I've looked at this report. I'm not sure why I keep staring at it," I mumble after several frustrating minutes.

"Since the words have remained consistent, maybe your gut is telling you something."

I glance up, smiling that he's making a point about trusting my earlier instincts with Mina when his comment hits me from another perspective. "Consistency! It wasn't the report, but the location."

"In what way?"

I realize he's acting as my sounding board, but his perceptive skills are strong, so maybe a back and forth could help. "The first bomb/igniter was taped to the edge of my tire rim, which would've put a hole in my tire, but the second igniter was put on the gas tank flap...a much deadlier, but also a more obvious place."

"Ah, I see. You're wondering why the person changed the location they put the bomb."

"And also *when* they did it, because where it was located—right there on the outside of the vehicle—

would've been much easier to discover, even if it was just a little over two inches long." I retrieve my phone and call the office. "Hey, Elijah, can you do me a favor and queue up all the church street footage we have from the night of the bombing? I know you've reviewed it, but I'd like to do so as well. Thanks, we'll be there in five minutes."

I hang up, anticipating scanning the videos with a keener eye. As Den turns on the road that'll lead us to the office, two loud splats hit the windshield, sending something like black ink or paint scattering across the glass.

"Bloody hell!" Den hits the breaks and as we screech to a halt, I'm glad the road is clear of cars at the moment. He immediately flicks on the windshield wipers, but the wiper fluid only smears the black mess, instead of cleaning it off.

Punching the door locks, he starts to dial a number when smoke begins to billow through the vents. "Gas," he mutters and drops his phone in his lap to turn off the internal vent button at the same time he hands me his pocket scarf. "Cover your nose and mouth, then call Sebastian."

While he proceeds to shut all the vents, I cover my nose and mouth with the cloth and reach for the phone in my lap, but it must've slid off the paperwork onto the floor when he hit the brakes. Bending down, I blindly grope for my phone, the toxic smoke stinging my eyes. I still haven't found it when Den pulls on my shoulder to get my attention.

"Talia," he says, sounding groggy. I take a short breath and try to keep from breathing in the gas as I straighten. Den shoves something toward me. "Hide this on you somewhere it won't be discovered."

As I take what feels like a pen, Den wheezes a couple of times, then slumps forward, losing consciousness.

"Den!" I drop the cloth and quickly tuck the pen inside my bra against the underwire, then turn and try to pull Den's limp body back against his seat. The smoke has made me so weak, it takes a couple attempts before I succeed. "Can you hear me?"

The inside of the car is completely filled with smoke now, making my eyes water and my lungs feel like they're on fire. I blindly lift Den's head back against the headrest, then slide my fingers down to his throat. I'm relieved his pulse feels strong under my fingers, but I'm woozy and my arms are too weak to shake him hard enough to wake him.

Everything feels like it's moving in slow motion and fire licks my lungs with the need for oxygen. Just as I shake my head to stay conscious, a heavy thump hits my window. The car rocks with another hit and I gulp in a gasp of pain when flying glass stings the side of my face. I intuitively turn away, my vision dimming.

CHAPTER SIXTEEN

Sebastian

"Slow your roll!" Banks throws a hand up and his dark eyes shift between Calder and me. "You think I had something to do with that bomb going off?"

"You threatened me the day before." I narrow my gaze on the picture in his hand. "Your girlfriend helped you escape the scene by using her car to block our pursuit, and Vinny Karras just gave you up as the person who bought the igniter that caused the gas tank to explode. Yeah, I'd say you're pretty fucked, Banks."

"Well, I'd say this reeks of a setup, because that what's going on," he says as he reaches into his pocket.

"Keep your hands still," Calder barks, holding his gun higher.

"Chill, Blake number two. I'm calling my girl. Sierra

can at least clear up where she was when the bomb went off."

"It's Calder," he snaps, then nods to Banks. "Move slow or you'll find out how accurate my aim is."

"Put it on speaker," I tell Banks.

He nods and we all listen to the phone ring four times before it goes to voicemail. "This is Sierra. I'm out blowing *all* the boys. Hahahaha! I'm just joking, Banksy. You know what to do."

When her voicemail beeps, Banks says, "Hey, babe. Call me back ASAP." Hanging up, he dials another number and tenses as he glances my way. "Paulo might know where she is. They both work at the Crazy Horse club." When Paulo's phone goes to voicemail too, Banks leaves him a message. "Hey, Paulo, forget that errand I asked you to run. I need you back here now."

"Two down. Ready for your third strike," I say in an impatient tone.

Setting his lips in a line of annoyance, Banks punches another number with vengeance. It rings and rings, then he hangs up and snaps his fingers at the young guy beside him. "Call Vinny's number."

His phone rings and he holds his hand up to the kid, telling him to wait while he answers. "Paulo, are you heading back?"

"No, man. I just got to the store. I'll just grab what's needed then—"

"I want you back here now," Banks bellows.

"What's going on, Banks?" Paulo asks in a calm tone.

Banks's gaze shifts between Calder and me. "Do you know if Sierra had to work? I can't get in touch with her."

"I'm not sure. I've had a few days off."

Banks blows out a frustrated breath. "What was I doing on Saturday night?"

"I don't know. What were you doing? I was out, remember."

"What do I *usually* do on Saturday nights?"

"Well, you usually have a beer with your uncle." As Banks shoots me an "I told you so" look, Paulo says, "Except you left early."

Confusion flickers in Bank's eyes. "No, I didn't."

"Yes, you did. You got mad at the server about the bill."

"I didn't leave early." Banks shakes his head, his forehead furrowed in frustration. "You weren't even there."

"You told me about it later. Maybe you were too drunk to remember?"

Banks opens his mouth to speak, but Paulo continues, "Listen, I'm already here, so I'm grabbing what we need. Then I've got some other errands to run. Be back later."

When Paulo hangs up, Banks grunts and nods to the kid beside him to complete the call. Once the kid dials Vinny's number, Banks snatches his phone and puts it on speaker.

"Vinny's Electronics, what can I help you with?"

"You can tell me why the fuck you're lying about me buying certain parts in your store, Vinny!" Banks barks.

"Sorry, I can't talk right now, Banks. A customer just walked in."

"Answer me, right now—"

Banks growls at the distinctive click and throws the phone against the wall across the room. I raise my eyebrow as the cell bursts into pieces. "And strike three."

"How can you not see this is a set up?" Banks rails, flinging his arms wide.

"Seems it's your word against Vinny's," I say. "Why would he lie?"

Banks puffs his chest up. "Exactly, why would he lie?"

Narrowing my gaze on him, I pull out my phone and call the office. "Hey, Elijah. I need you to dig a bit deeper into Vinny Karras. Call me right back."

As soon as I hang up, Banks crosses his arms and stares me down. "I think you're asking the wrong question."

I scowl at him. "What question should I be asking?"

"Whoever is setting me up...why did they drag *you* into it?"

I don't like Banks trying to mess with my head, but if there's even an ounce of truth to what he's saying, then whoever blew up that limo is still out there with devious planning skills. That makes them even more dangerous.

I call Talia's number and when it goes to voicemail,

I glance at Calder and quickly tap the number for Den's phone. The moment I get his voicemail, I hang up and call Elijah back. "Before you work on the other, I need you to ping Talia's cell. Something's not right."

"She was on her way back to the office." A pause, but that was longer than she said it would take. Let me check…" A couple seconds pass. "Her phone's not even a mile from the office, but that's weird. The signal's on the road and not moving. I also just pinged Den's phone. It's the same."

"You're closest. Get there now! We're on our way."

I nod to Calder and tuck my gun away. Just before I reach the front door, Banks says, "What about me?"

I follow Calder out. "I'll deal with you later."

"I'm being set up! Hey, you own that security company. You can help me—"

I close the door, cutting him off and instantly dial Den's number again, my heart beating hard as his phone rings several times.

Banks yanks the door open and follows us out, his voice raised. "Wait? Deal with me later? What the hell's that supposed to mean, Blackie?"

My phone rings and I quickly answer, barking into the phone at Elijah, "Tell me she's okay!"

"That depends. You didn't do your job."

Paulo. Ice slides down my back and I halt my fast stride in the middle of the sidewalk. Barely resisting the urge to chew the little shit's head off, I say, "Which was?"

"Banks is in my way."

Calder looks at me with concern when I glance back at Banks. "What do you want?" I say, turning so Banks can't see my expression.

"Fuck you!" Banks yells, then slams his door in the background.

"You want your wife back? Take out Banks, permanently. Isn't that what you SEALs do?"

"Touch her at all and you'll learn that monsters truly exist."

"You do your part, she'll stay safe. Do you understand?"

Is he so delusional that he thinks I won't go after him later? Either that or he has help. "Yes," I grit out.

"Good. Now go back in there and take care of him. Once I see video proof that it's been done, I'll let Talia go."

I punch the End button and say in a low voice to Calder, "Back me up on this," before I turn around and take the stairs to bang on the door."

Banks pulls the door open and yells, "What do want now?"

"For you to die." Throwing a fast, hard punch, I send his big body slamming to the foyer floor.

Following me inside, Calder kicks the door closed and draws his gun, his voice booming throughout the room as he addresses the guys ready to jump to Banks's defense. "Stay back. This is between Sebastian and Banks."

I bend on one knee and grab Banks's shirt, then get right in his face and say loud enough for the tense men in the room to hear what's going on, "Paulo is your traitor. He has Talia. In exchange for her safe return, he wants you dead."

Banks's eyes slit in anger and he grabs my fist on his shirt with one hand as he tries to punch me with his other. I quickly deflect his swing and pound my fist into his shoulder to keep him still. As he moans in pain, I snap, "You're going to do exactly what I say. Is that clear?"

Banks grits his teeth and spits blood onto the floor. "Fuck you! You broke my nose, motherfucker!"

"Shut up!" Smashing my hand against his hurt nose, I grunt my satisfaction at his growl of pain, then wipe my hand off down the front of his shirt. "Where's your liquor?"

"What?" Banks's eyes widen, looking at me like I've lost my mind.

"Might as well celebrate your impending demise," I say, twisting my hand in his shirt once more.

"Kitchen," the young teen whispers, eyes wide.

I glance up at the others staring at me with a mixture of fear and fascination as if they're not sure what they're seeing is really happening. "If you three want to survive this, do as Calder tells you."

Standing, I use Banks's shirt to haul him to his feet. He struggles and tries to fight me, but I pinch a nerve on his shoulder. The second he drops to his knees, I turn and tell Calder what I need from him. "Get moving," I bark at Banks's guys, then release Banks to grab a straight-backed chair near a side table.

Calder lifts his gun, his expression supportive and determined. "You heard him, back in the kitchen now!"

"Get out of my fucking house!" Banks hobbles to stand and tries to rush me, but I swing the chair, forcing him to jump back.

When I send it into the big window near the door and glass shatters, raining everywhere, Banks snarls, "You're going to pay for this!"

I get right in his face, my voice lethal with my worry for Talia. "I'm going to burn this fucking place to the ground."

CHAPTER SEVENTEEN

Talia

"**W**ake up!" a man's snaps in my ear right before a splash of ice cold water hits my face.

I gasp and my eyes fly open. I'm sitting in a chair with my wrists bound together in my lap. I bend my fingers around and feel a hard plastic band, probably a Zip Tie. Everything is blurry and I blink several times trying to get my vision to focus.

A man is standing in front of me. He's dark-headed, but I can't make out any features other than his overall shape. My head feels like it's full of fuzz and my mouth is so dry I actually lick the water off my lips just so I have enough spit to swallow.

"Water," I croak and a bottle is pressed against my lips. I drink several gulps before it's taken away. My heart races once my basic survival needs are met. *Where am I? Who has taken me? Why?* I open and close my eyes several times, but my vision never clears. Panicking, my breathing ramps even faster than my heart's beating. "Why can't I see?"

He moves closer and waves a hand in front of my face. "You can't see me?"

He thinks I can't see at all? I try not to track his hand movement and keep my gaze slightly lowered as I shake my head and exaggerate my worry to I'm-freaking-out mode. I twist in the chair, looking left and then right. "What's wrong with my vision?"

"Must be the gas we used," he mutters.

We? He's working with someone. *Why does his voice sound familiar?* "Who are you? What do you want?" I say in a much stronger voice than I feel.

"Just calm down. Once Banks is taken care of, you'll be fine."

The mention of Banks gives me a context for the voice. Paulo. Banks's second in command. Is he here on Banks's orders? Pretending I don't know who I'm talking to won't help me get answers, so I say, "Paulo?"

"The one and only."

I fold my hands together to force myself to remain calm. He's already killed once. I don't need to rile him. "Was that bombing that happened outside the church some kind of screwed up revenge against Sebastian? What do you mean once Banks is taken care of?"

"Revenge?" the guy snorts and pulls a seat up in front of me. "No, Talia, this is about what I *deserve*. Sebastian has been targeted, but not in the way you think. Banks needs to retire and let the young bloods lead. Under my leadership, the boys will thrive and be what they once were before Banksy went soft."

Standing, he shoves his hands in his pants pockets and paces behind the chair. "What kind of crew doesn't carry guns? Or run drugs in their neighborhood?" He pauses to put his hands on the back of the chair and expels an annoyed snort. "Banks's Boys are the only fucking ones! We may as well be a boy band. It's a fucking miracle our whole crew hasn't been gunned down before now."

"You don't have guns in your house at all?" That does surprise me.

"Of course we have guns, but Banks made it a rule to keep them put away and that we're not allowed to be strapped. He said it's the fastest way to get ourselves killed." He lets out a derisive laugh. "I'll bet Derrick, who was shot and killed coming back from a club last month, would argue with that pussy philosophy."

Paulo slams his fist onto the table next to me, making me jump. "We need to be stronger. We need to be armed, not just with knives. We should fucking *own* the neighborhood, not just look like we do. All this is about to change!"

"How do you plan to change it?"

"By getting rid of Banks."

"Why does he have to go?" Anxious, I lean forward and something jabs into my breast. Then I remember Den's pen that I'd put in my bra. I'm not sure what it does, but I feel better just knowing it's there.

Paulo steps forward and puts a hand on my shoulder. Pushing me back against the seat, he waves a gun in front of me. "You can't see it, but I'm holding a gun. Stay there if you don't want to get hurt." Snorting, he backs away and sets the gun on the table. "It's not like you can see to get very far."

Since he didn't answer my question, I give him my opinion anyway. "Killing Banks won't get you what you want. You know his boys are loyal to him. What makes you think they'll be loyal to you after you kill their leader?"

He *tsks*. "I'm not the one who's going to kill him. Your husband's going to do it for me."

"What?" When I shake my head in fast jerks, my stomach lurches, but my vision is also starting to clear. "Sebastian will *never* do that." As Paulo's spiked, short hair takes shape, I lower my gaze so he can't see that I'm trying to take in my surroundings: door with a flip latch, a bed to my left, window and small table to the right. Water damage along the walls near the door and the faint smell of mildew in the air. We're in a motel room.

"Oh, but he's already agreed. I'm just waiting for

confirmation."

The idea Sebastian would kill an innocent person to save me makes me feel light-headed. *Stop thinking about it. Trust in him and stay focused.* "You said *we* earlier," I say. "Who is we?"

Paulo laughs and sits back down in the chair facing me. "Let's just say I'll have the very best connections. Not only that, but I'll be running his guns and drugs through my neighborhood. It's going to be a perfect, untouchable partnership."

Untouchable? Is that why he doesn't seem to be worried that Sebastian will come after him? Is this guy mafia? Or God, do they plan to get rid of Sebastian too? I tilt my head and stare slightly away from his face so he can't see my concern growing. "If you're so untouchable, why didn't you take Banks out yourself?"

"I don't kill. Banks and Blackie have history. I figured your husband might even enjoy this job."

No, you're weak and you'd rather have others do your dirty work for you. "But you've already killed!" It's hard not to jerk my gaze to his, but I catch myself before I make that mistake. "Isabel Blake is dead because of you."

Paulo looks away and shakes his head. "That wasn't how it was supposed to go down."

"You put the bomb on the gas tank flap, so of course a spark will blow the gas. What else did you expect would happen?"

Paulo starts to speak but he gets a text. Glancing down at his phone, he looks at me, a sudden grin on his face as he reads me the text. "Gun shots at Banks's house. Men yelling. Neighbors must've called the police. Sirens on their way." Paulo's phone begins to beep with an incoming video call.

"Showtime!" he says, dark eyes lighting up as he turns his chair around. Sitting beside me close enough for "selfie" mode, he hits the button to answer, but quickly flips the camera so all the caller sees is the dingy hotel wall.

Sebastian appears to be standing on what looks like the porch of Banks's house. Glass is everywhere under his feet. He looks pissed as hell. "I want proof that my wife is unharmed."

"You were only supposed to call me once the job was done," Paulo snaps, his voice jumping an octave. "If I don't see proof in two seconds…" He picks up the gun and moves it before the front-facing camera."

Sebastian's face sets in hard lines, suppressed fury evident. I'm so worried, I call out. "I'm here, Sebastian. Please don't do this!"

Paulo quickly sets the gun down on the table, then clamps his hand painfully over my mouth and chin, locking me in place. "Enough! Is it done? Show me."

Sebastian pans the camera over the porch and Banks is laying on his back, half inside the doorway. Eyes staring sightlessly upward, his nose and face a bloody mess and his shirt torn and matted with way too much blood.

I gasp behind Paulo's hand, tears filling my eyes. *No, Sebastian! This can't be true.*

"I've done my part, but to assure you do yours and let Talia go…" Turning the camera back to himself, Sebastian's blue eyes narrow as he pans the camera back some and we see Calder hand him a lit Molotov cocktail.

"What the fuck!" Paulo yells, pounding his fist on the arm of my chair. "That's not part of the deal!"

"The house and everyone inside is now yours." Sebastian tosses the bottle inside the house through the broken window. A burst of flames quickly licks up from the floor and along the windowsill as dark smoke billows out the window. "Release Talia and leave now if you want to save it."

The moment Sebastian hangs up, I grab the gun and throw it as hard as I can at the window. The glass shatters in a loud crash and Paulo whirls on me, fury stamped on his face.

I duck, evading his swinging fist, and bolt for the door.

He grabs my hair and yanks me back. "You saw that, you lying bitch!"

Just as he hauls me against him, wrapping his arm tight around my neck, a man says in a harsh tone, "Let her go, right *now*."

Den and another man with dark hair and piercing gray eyes stand just outside the broken window, their guns drawn.

Paulo lets out a maniacal laugh. "You're not going to do shit. Sebastian will kill you both if anything happens to her. She goes with me or I'll snap her neck where we stand," he says, tightening his arm. "Move, Talia!"

Unfortunately, he's just short enough to hunch and keep his head and body behind mine. While he shuffles us toward the door, I fold my bound wrists to my chest and work the pen from the bottom of my bra while Paulo's distracted.

When Den sees the pen curled tight in my hands, he nods and lowers his gun. "Let them go, Elijah," he says in a calm tone. Elijah glances his way and frowns, but then lowers his weapon as well.

The moment we walk through the doorway onto the sidewalk, I swing my bound hands in an upward arc, aiming the pen right for Paulo's head.

Paulo lets out a horrific yell and releases me to fall against the wall, grabbing his injured, bleeding face. "My eye! My eye! You bitch. I'll kill everyone you care about!"

Still pumped on adrenaline, I shout, "Don't threaten my family." I turn with my arm raised, ready to lash out at him once more.

Den captures my arm before I can connect. Pulling me away, he traps me against his solid frame with an arm around my shoulder. "You're okay, Talia. He's down."

Keeping his gun trained on Paulo, Elijah pulls his

phone out, his eyes sliding over to me with wary respect. "Remind me to never piss you off."

"Nice to finally meet you in person too, Elijah," I say with an embarrassed half-smile. He really did just see me at my absolute worst.

While Elijah rattles off the address to the police, Den releases me to walk into the motel room and retrieve a couple hand towels from the bathroom. Hauling Paulo to his feet, Den shoves a towel in Paulo's hands, then walks over to me, holding the other one—doused with soap and water—out, his tone soft but proud as he takes the pen from my shaking hands. "This pen was meant to be used as a tracker."

"I improvised." My bravado falters when I glance down to wipe my hands on the towel. The sight of Paulo's bright red blood brings home how lucky I was that Den found me, making my legs shake a little. I'm so glad I didn't have to find out what Paulo would've done if I hadn't thrown his gun through the window. Den's beside me instantly, holding my arm until I nod that my legs aren't going to fail me.

Exhaling, he squeezes my arm. "Are you sure you're steady now?"

"I'm good." I study his face. He looks worried and a bit tired. "Are *you* okay? It took some time for my vision to fully return once I woke up."

He nods. "Whatever they used to gas us was high tech

and something I've never seen." Pulling his phone out of his pocket, he hands it to me. "Sebastian wants to talk to you."

Both relieved and anxious, I walk away from the men and put the phone to my ear. "Were you on the phone the whole time?"

"Of course. Are you truly okay, Talia? That backstabbing little shit deserves to be shot."

His protective comment makes me feel warm inside. "I'm fine."

"I still want you checked out by an EMT when the ambulance gets there. Calder and I are on our way to you now."

The sound of him shifting gears finally filters through. "Please tell me that you didn't really kill Banks, Sebastian," I whisper.

"I will do whatever it takes to keep you safe, Little Red."

Tears mist in my eyes, but I hold them back. "But not like this."

"I won't say I didn't enjoy getting in some well overdue punches. Banks sure as hell deserved them, but no...he's very much alive."

Gulping my relief, I glance back to see the ambulance has arrived ahead of the police. "And the house and everyone else?"

"No one was harmed. It was a contained fire. We

planned it to look much worse from the outside than it was. We knew we were being watched."

"Someone was feeding Paulo info via text. Paulo intended to run guns and drugs for a partner. I hope Paulo will give up whoever his partner is now that he's going to be arrested."

"Tell Elijah to grab Paulo's phone before the police get there. We might be able to trace it back to his partner ourselves."

I smirk when I see Den slip Elijah Paulo's cell. That's what he was doing when he handed Paulo that towel. "Already on it. I'm glad you're coming."

"Be there in five, sweetheart."

Hanging up, I exhale a deep breath that Sebastian didn't have to cross a line on my behalf, and that we've at least caught one of the people responsible for Isabel's death.

CHAPTER EIGHTEEN

Talia

"*Want* a slice of pepperoni, veggie, or loaded with meat?" Sebastian asks me across the kitchen table in the BLACK Security office.

"Pepperoni," I say, holding my paper plate out.

"You sure you don't want a beer, Talia?" Calder asks as he grabs one from the fridge.

"If I have a beer, Sebastian will be carrying me out of here. It's been a long day."

"Let's try that some time. I think it'd be fun to cart you home drunk off your ass." Sebastian shoots me a wicked grin before he gulps down half his bottle of water in one long swig.

"I'm with, Talia." Calder snorts his agreement and lifts the bottle in salute to me. "It's not every day I think my cousin has gone off the deep end."

"How *did* you two convince Banks to go along with your plan?" I ask once I swallow my bite of pizza.

"I didn't really give him a choice," Sebastian says, tossing his plate into the trash.

Calder points to his cousin with his pizza slice. "That, and the fact he wanted to screw Paulo over once he learned of his betrayal."

Nodding my understanding, I shift my gaze to Den and Elijah, who are so busy eating, they haven't said a word. "Once you two vacuums are done consuming a whole pizza each, we need to compare notes from the day and see if we missed anything."

Just as Calder lifts the beer to open it, Sebastian says, "You probably should limit yourself to one, Cald. We're expected at the precinct first thing tomorrow morning to make our statements."

"Might as well skip it then." Calder stares at his beer with a forlorn expression, then stands to return it to the fridge.

Crumpling my napkin, I say, "Paulo has a partner. He said that his partner wanted him to run drugs and guns through his neighborhood. And that he would be untouchable."

"We know that they used tech beyond anything I've seen to gas us," Den says. "I checked with my UK contacts and they hadn't heard of anything like that either. They're definitely connected to someone with money or have access to high tech equipment."

"Who else from Banks's Boys or contacts were working with Paulo?" I ask, looking at Sebastian and Calder.

"Vinny the shop owner," Calder says. "And Banks's girlfriend, Sierra."

"We haven't been able to find Sierra." Sebastian looks at Elijah. "What did you find out about Vinny?"

"Nothing. His bank accounts seem squeaky clean. No large sums of money have been deposited." Elijah wipes pizza sauce from his lips and swallows some soda. "Unless he's hiding money under other IDs, that's all I could find."

"You don't have any idea why Vinny threw Banks under the bus?" I look at Sebastian.

He shakes his head. "Vinny blew Banks off when he tried to confront him about it earlier."

I frown and gnaw my bottom lip. "How well does Banks know Vinny? He might give us some insight."

"Can't hurt to ask. What's his number, Talia?"

I look up Banks's number in my contacts and Sebastian dials it, putting his phone on speaker.

Two rings later, Banks grates into the phone. "Who is this?"

"It's Sebastian. I have a question."

"What are we, *besties* now?"

"Bite me, Banks. This is important."

"You'd *better* be calling me to tell me you've written a

check to cover all this damage."

"That 'damage' saved your life. Now shut it and listen. Paulo was working with a man who wanted Paulo to take your place so he could run drugs and guns through your neighborhood. You've still got an enemy out there. Now that Paulo can't follow through with his plans, this guy will look for someone else to take his place."

"Hell no, he's *not* bringing that shit in my neighborhood! Who the fuck *is* this guy?"

"If you don't want that to happen, then talk to me about Vinny. What do you know about him? Why would he lie about you?"

"I have no clue why. Vinny did have a gambling problem in the past. Ran up a good bit of debt. Thought he'd gotten clean though."

"Maybe not." Sebastian looks at Elijah. "Go back a bit further in his finances."

"Are you talking to me?" Banks says.

"No, you're on speaker. Members of my BLACK Security team are here, helping me dig into this."

Once Elijah pushes his plate away and then opens his laptop, I speak up. "Hey, Banks. It's Talia. Something's been bothering me. Did you get my message to you in the pizza delivery box?"

"What message? The last time I heard from you was that voicemail about the article being delayed."

"Talia tried to warn you about the police, Banks. The

Tribune called the police without her knowledge."

I smile at my husband, appreciating that he wanted to set the record straight, but that wasn't why I was asking. "If you didn't get my message, then how did you manage to avoid getting arrested for having the painting in your house?"

"Paulo gave me the heads up the police were coming and what they'd be looking for early in the morning. I almost ripped his head off when I found out the painting was stolen. He promised me that it was a one-time deal and he was done with that kind of stuff."

Sebastian and I exchange a glance. "I didn't send my message until lunchtime, so who warned Paulo?"

"I never got your message, Talia. I knew because we have a police contact," Banks grudgingly admits.

"What?" Sebastian leans forward at this news. "Who?"

"Don't know. He was Paulo's contact and said it was best if he only interacted with one of us, so I didn't push to learn his name."

"Fucking hell. What if Paulo's partner is a cop, or a cop working with Paulo's partner? Paulo won't make it to trial if we don't get him protection."

"You think I give a shit if Paulo makes it to trial?"

"A dead man can't tell us who his partner is, Banks!" Sebastian grabs my phone and walks away to make a call.

"If a police officer is involved with this whole thing, that would explain Paulo's access to that high-tech ink used to gas us earlier," Den says. "Think about all the items that get seized during raids and entered into evidence."

"British guy's there too?" Banks snorts. "He's a damn big guy."

"Still right here," Den says in a dry tone.

"Speaking of evidence," Elijah says in a low voice to me. "Phil dropped off an evidence package with your necklace earlier today. It's in Sebastian's office."

When I nod, he looks back down at his laptop and taps on his keys. "Okay, I went back a bit further on Vinny, and yep, he drew down his savings account to the tune of forty-thousand dollars over a period of three months less than two years ago. And then the account stopped bleeding."

"How are you seeing his finances?"

"Owing a huge debt like that can shift loyalties on a dime," Calder says over Banks's question.

"Are you saying you don't think he got clean?" Banks says, his suspicious tone sharpening.

"When have you ever known a gambler to just stop cold turkey?" Calder answers. "They're either beat to a pulp and forced to pay up, or they pay the debt and finally join groups to get help."

"Or, the other option is...someone takes care of their debt and they straighten out their lives in gratitude." I glance Sebastian's way, thinking about what my husband did for Phil.

"Most people don't erase debt without an agenda,"

Sebastian says as he returns to the table. "To Calder's point, having his debt wiped clean would explain Vinny's sudden about face with you, Banks."

"Yeah it would," Banks grouses. "Sierra hasn't shown her face. I'm pretty sure she was hooking up with Paulo. She won't be back, but looks like I'll have to pay Vinny a visit tomorrow."

"No, stay away from Vinny," Sebastian says in a harsh tone. "You could tip Paulo's partner off and we'll lose our advantage. Right now the guy doesn't know that Paulo told us his plans."

"What did the police say?" Calder asks before Banks can argue.

"The police chief is moving Paulo to a secure location with a couple trusted guards, but he only agreed to do that if we all came in tonight to make our statements."

"The police already have my statement," Banks interjects. "Are we done with the twenty questions now?"

"Yeah, we're done. And, Banks...I shouldn't have to remind you not to repeat anything we've talked about or it could blow this case, right?"

"Got it, Blackie. The next time I hear from you, it better be you telling me you're sending a check."

"Blackie?" Elijah mouths to Sebastian, curious amusement dancing is his gray eyes.

Ignoring Elijah, Sebastian snorts and says, "It's in the mail," then hangs up.

"What time are we going to the station?" Calder asks, as he types out a text on his phone. "Cass is on her way back from visiting her parents and planned to stop by here for a slice."

"How far out is she?" Sebastian asks.

"About fifteen minutes."

"We'll wait for her." Turning to Elijah, he asks, "What's the latest on Paulo's phone?"

"Been running a diagnostic on it. I'll go get it."

He starts to stand, but I wave him back into his seat. "I'll grab it on the way back from Sebastian's office. I want to see just how badly damaged my necklace is."

"It's at my cubicle workstation, not in my office. Bring the cord too."

"Do you need the lights?" Sebastian calls as I leave the room.

"No, I'm good."

On my way to Sebastian's office, I wind my way through the dim rows of cubicles until I find Elijah's workstation and Paulo's phone. "Who knew the guy had his own office? No wonder I hadn't seen him yet," I mutter to myself as I unhook the phone from Elijah's desktop computer but leave the USB cord attached.

Once I reach Sebastian's office and locate the envelope with my name on it, there's enough light from the streetlights outside to allow me to see just how bad off my necklace is. It's truly beyond repair. Sniffing back unshed tears, I drop the necklace back in the envelope and slide the envelope into my purse. With a sad sigh, I wind the phone's USB cord around my hand as I start back across the office space toward the hall and the lunchroom beyond. The guys are laughing uproariously about something, and their amusement makes me pick up my pace. I could use a good laugh to lift my spirits right now.

A click of the Emergency exit stairwell door just ahead draws my attention and I instantly slow my steps. *Is Cass early? Why is she coming in the back way?*

When a man walks through the door, I move next to the wall near the copier hoping he won't see me. His chest is the only part of him lit up by the dim lighting and he's right in my path to get back to the lunchroom. He takes a couple of steps into the room and as he turns to scan over the cubicles and lifts his hand with something in it, the phone in my hand lights up with an incoming text.

Test

I glance up to see if he noticed the light. *Oh shit,* it's the detective, Phil Mayhew, who was working the limo bombing. He turns in my direction, his gaze narrowed on me.

"Give that to me," he hisses and starts toward me with determined strides, pulling a gun from underneath his jacket.

Heart racing, I pivot and bolt for Sebastian's office. The only reason Phil would risk coming here is if the phone contains evidence that'll tie him to Paulo. He must've traced its signal.

I drop the phone as I quickly turn and shut the door, but the dead bolt doesn't budge, so I throw my back against the door and wedge my shoes on the carpet to keep him out.

A heavy thump shoves against the wood behind me twice, then stops.

Just as I exhale a shaky breath, several light pinging sounds hit the glass that runs along the top half of the wall to my right.

I need to warn Sebastian, but the damn phone bounced away from me when it dropped on the carpet.

Phil must have a silencer on his gun. I squeeze my eyes shut, ever so thankful for my husband's paranoia. The bulletproof glass seems to be holding. The pings continue until all I hear is the click of an empty gun.

A couple seconds pass and then the door shoves toward me once and then again. Each time inching my feet forward. My pulse thunders and I feel slightly faint. I take a deep breath, while my legs shake to hold the door closed. At this rate, he'll be in here in seconds.

This button is all it takes to lock down this office in seconds, Talia.

Sebastian's comment about the office security system comes to me, and my gaze zeros on his desk. I just need to push the button underneath. But I'll have to leave the door unblocked long enough to get to it. *How the hell am I going to do that?*

Glancing down at my toes straining against the edges of my wedge sandals instantly reminds me of Cass reprimanding me for not wearing toenail polish with open-toed shoes. *She's going to give me so much shit tonight...Oh God*, tonight! *Cass could walk into this standoff at any moment!* I have to find a way to get to that button before she arrives. As I continue to stare at my shoes, my chest tightening with worry, I realize that I might be able to buy myself a tiny bit of time.

Two more hits against the door and Phil's angry growl of frustration is enough to make me take the chance. Resetting my footing, I quickly bend my leg and remove my shoe, then return my bare foot to the carpet. Now I just have to wait for him to try once again.

My feet slip with the next powerful slam of his body against the door. I grit my teeth and use all my strength to keep him out. The moment the second hit happens, I quickly drop to my knees and slide the toe of my shoe under the space between the door and the carpet, pushing the thick wedge heel forward as much as possible to jam the door closed.

I don't even look behind me as I quickly crawl over to the desk. *God, please let Cass still be on the road.* My gaze shifts back to the door as I push the lockdown button several times and hope like hell it has an alarm attached to it.

At the same time the bolt on the door electronically flips into place, a loud siren begins to blare throughout the office.

Pumping a victory fist that the traitorous detective is now trapped in an office with no bullets and a group of well-trained alpha men bearing down on him, I slump over to my side on the carpet and exhale an exhausted breath of sheer relief.

CHAPTER NINETEEN

Sebastian

"So...*Blackie,* huh?" Elijah says the moment Talia leaves to retrieve Paulo's phone. His amused, gray gaze flicks to me across the table. "What *else* don't we know about your past, Bash?"

I ignore his dig. "You mean like we still don't know what hometown you're from?"

When Den's eyebrows elevate, Calder gestures to Elijah. "Apparently he was hatched from an egg."

Laughter rounds the table. "He has a mother. Speaking of which..." I pause and address Elijah. "When are you going to tell her that you work for a security firm and not a mail order company? Hell, for that matter...does she even know you're a SEAL?"

Rolling his eyes at our ribbing, Elijah flips a pen back

and forth around his thumb. "It's just easier—"

"Not to let her know you're costing me a fucking fortune?"

Elijah flashes a Cheshire grin. "I'm worth every penny."

"Enough to warrant *two* office spaces?"

I don't miss my cousin's sarcasm, but Calder also hasn't witnessed Elijah's wizardry firsthand. He'll change his tune when he does. "If you'd rather have a cubicle, Cald, I'm sure your *brother* would love to have your office to use whenever he's around."

Cutting a quick glare my way, Calder leans back in his chair, then folds his arms as a smug look slowly spreads across his face. "I'm not letting you bait me, since I'll be moving into your office soon enough. The first thing I'm going to do is take out that plain-ass glass window and add something more visually appealing. Not sure what though, maybe glass blocks."

"Trust me, it's functional," I say.

"Why is Calder planning to take over your office?" Elijah frowns, his gaze darting suspiciously between Calder and me. "Where are you going?"

"I'm not going anywhere. Calder mistakenly believes he knows what his fiancé is thinking. I've warned him he couldn't be more wrong."

"*When* I win, Bash's office is mine," Calder says, flashing a wide grin.

Den barks out a laugh, amusement dancing in his gaze.

"Might as well prepare to lose, Calder."

"Nuh uh, I've got this one lock—"

The sudden blaring of the security alarm jacks my pulse and sends me vaulting across the table before anyone can move. I bolt for the door just as everyone else jumps to their feet. "The alarm system will alert the police, but call them directly too," I say to Calder, then rush out the door into the dark hall, my only thought to get to Talia.

A loud crash reaches my ears above the blaring alarm just as I hit the end of the hall. I round the corner to see a man slamming the wheels of a swivel chair down on the emergency exit's door handle. My gaze narrows to angry slits.

Phil.

I quickly scan the dark office space, looking for Talia, the siren's din in my ears jacking my tension. When I don't see her, the white blinking lights in the ceiling corners turns a violent shade of red with my worried fury. Clenching my fists, I bellow, "Where the fuck is my wife?"

At the same time Phil casts angry eyes my way, he throws the chair in my direction and then takes off around the cubicles, running toward the back of the office.

My line of sight shifts ahead to my closed office door. *Is Talia in there? Is she okay? What if the lock didn't engage?* When the flashing lights reflect on the spider-webbed, bullet-riddled glass on my office wall, I know I can't wait for the guys who are pounding the floor just behind me.

From my position at the opposite corner of the room, there's only one path that'll possibly get me to Phil before he reaches my office door: straight through.

"Go around," I yell to the men just before I take a running leap onto Theo's desk, then immediately vault onto the corner edge of his cubicle wall. The wall wobbles under my weight, but I don't slow my momentum. I jump to the next desk and the cubicles begin to collapse like dominoes. Leaping over a falling wall, I hit another desk. My shoes barely touch the surface before I vault to an adjacent desk until I'm almost upon Phil.

I land on the last leaning cubicle wall wedged between fallen walls and a desk. Just as it starts to topple, I spring off it, throwing my full weight toward the deceitful cop right before he reaches the door. On my downward arc, I lock my hands on his shoulders. The jarring impact sends him to the floor.

Phil grunts from the hit, but he manages to dive out of my way before I can get a punch in. I quickly roll to my feet. Pivoting, I start toward him as he stumbles to stand, but he draws his gun and takes a step back. "Stay the hell still, Sebastian," he grits out, glaring at me with caged, desperate eyes.

Den, Calder, and Elijah freeze mid-run. Calder tightens his hand on his phone, his gaze jerking to me.

I know none of them had time to grab a gun and Den keeps his in his car when he's off-duty. "Shut that fucking alarm off, Calder," I call over the noise. Holding my hand up to silently tell the men to stand down, I turn back to Phil. "You get one chance to respond. Where the hell is my wife?" The alarm stops halfway through my last sentence, my deep voice a menacing bark of authority in the sudden silence.

"I'm not telling you shit," Phil says, his tone tense as the gun in his hand shakes slightly. "Unlock this goddamn place or I'll shoot you where you stand."

Movement in my periphery catches my attention. The sight of Talia's red hair through the damaged glass is so powerfully relieving I have to swallow to keep my face impassive. I can tell she's trying to say something but the room is sound proofed for privacy and the glass too damaged for me to read her lips to make out what she's saying. She must've quickly realized that, because she holds one hand up in the shape of a gun and then forms the letter O with the other hand.

O? What the hell is she trying to tell me?

"I'm not fucking kidding, Sebastian. I don't give a damn whose son you are. Unlock this fucking building now!"

From his position next to the door, Phil can't see Talia, who's now putting three fingers up, then two, then one. When she switches back to O, I finally get what she's been trying to say. The motherfucker is out of bullets!

Curling my lip in a sneer of disdain, I say, "You want

out?"

"Right fucking now!" Phil yells.

I let loose with a jabbing punch to his nose, then follow with a right hook to his jaw, gritting out, "Don't threaten my family, fucking *ever* again." The impact knocks him back a couple of steps. He instantly drops his gun, his expression one of shock as he teeters to remain standing.

Shaking his head to clear it, Phil growls his fury and starts toward me, but I spin into a roundhouse kick and send the bastard flying into the wall.

Once Phil slithers to the floor, knocked out cold, Den pulls his cell out and dials the police.

Calder's holding his phone, but his gaze is locked on the bullet holes in the glass window. "I promise to never discount your paranoia again."

"Told you it was functional." Taking his cell phone, I hit the button on the alarm system's control panel that unlocks my office door.

The moment the lock disengages, Talia pulls open the door and runs out, throwing herself into my arms.

I fold my arms around her and hold her close. Inhaling her sweet smell, I exhale slowly as I kiss her forehead. "Are you okay?"

She nods against my chest, then lifts her head to see Elijah nudging Phil with his foot. "Is he?"

"He's knocked out, but breathing," Elijah announces while kicking Phil's gun away.

Talia returns her gaze to me, a wry smile tilting her lips. "We're going to have to work on your Charades skills, Mister Black."

I chuckle and pull her even closer. "I'm always up for games with you, Little Red. In the meantime, would you like to share why you're only wearing one shoe?"

CHAPTER TWENTY

Talia

"Yes, sir," Sebastian says as he beeps his car and we walk across our apartment's underground parking lot to the elevator. "First thing in the morning the BLACK Security team will be in to make a full statement."

He slides his phone into his pocket and we step on the elevator. I wait for him to punch in our code before I speak. "I'm so glad you got the Chief to agree to wait until tomorrow morning. I'm so tired I might fall asleep before we get to our floor."

Sebastian hooks his arm around my shoulders and pulls me against his solid warmth. "A police officer's involvement and arrest adds a whole other layer to the investigation. Now internal affairs has to get involved. The Chief wants to tackle setting up the meetings in the right order and we'll sit down with him after we've all had a good night's sleep."

I look at his knuckles hanging over my shoulder and grimace at their roughed-up state. "You're going to need to put some ice on that."

"Beating the shit out of Phil was worth the pain," he says, curling his hand and flashing a dark smile.

His alpha ways frustrate just as much as they fascinate me, but I wouldn't have him any other way. "What did the Chief say? It sounds like you got some updates."

Sebastian nods as we reach our floor and step into our living room. "Once Paulo learned that Phil had been arrested, he started talking. He maintains that he never put the igniter on the gas tank flap. He said he only wanted to blow the tire, so that's where he put the device. He says that Phil must've moved it that night. According to him, Phil started that heist ring—the one that was responsible for that stolen art collection among other things—to fund his true desire to run his own drug and gun running business in the Lower East Side. What Phil didn't know was that Paulo kept one of the paintings they stole. It was Paulo's way to protect himself in case things went south."

"How would the painting protect him?"

Sebastian smirks. "Phil cut himself during one of the heists. His blood is embedded in the scrollwork of the frame. Turning on Phil could possibly reduce Paulo's sentence."

"Did Phil confess to moving the device?"

"I haven't gotten information on Phil's interrogation yet, but I can't imagine him admitting murdering Isabel, even if he was guilty. Either way, both men have enough charges against them to put them away for a long time."

I'm bothered by the fact Paulo claims Phil had to have moved the igniter. Even though it fits with what he told me...that he wasn't a killer. I will have to review the tapes from that night to appease that nagging doubt that something doesn't quite add up. Whether he's guilty of that part or not, I really don't like the idea that Paulo might get less time for turning on Phil. "I'm sorry about Phil turning out the way he did." I wrap my arm around my husband's waist and shake my head.

Sebastian gives a wry smile. "Who better to know how to bring a gambler like Vinny to his side than the guy who'd been through it with his own kid? Without Vinny lying about Banks's involvement in the threat against my family, I might never have gone after him."

"Well, I just hope Phil's betrayal doesn't stop you from helping others, Sebastian."

He curls his arm on my shoulders, pulling me fully against his solid frame. "That's what I have you for...to remind me to be human when the ugliness of the world closes in." Kissing my forehead, he lifts my chin up. "You impress the hell out of me in so many ways. What do you say to a Red and Black investigative team?"

My heart races, but I don't want to get my hopes up. "Are we talking about fiction? Or in real life?"

"I'm serious. You're such a natural, Talia, and we work so well together. I'd like you to come work with us at BLACK Security."

Before I can speak, he continues, "You'll have your own office, and I'll make sure you get enough downtime to write your books between cases." A cocky smile crooks his lips. "Maybe I'll even give you some inspiration for Aaron White. What do you say?"

I grin my happiness and wrap my arms around his neck. "It's about time you recognized that my awesome investigative skills have BLACK Security written all over them!"

"Your skills were never in question, sweetheart." His expression settles to a serious one. "I knew how much working for the Tribune meant to you, and I didn't want to take you away from that."

"Priorities shift," I say, shrugging. "By the way, I...um quit the other day. So this career opportunity comes at a perfect time for this jobless girl."

"What?" A dark scowl instantly forms around his mouth and he steps back to grip my shoulders. "Did they fire you? I'm going to—"

"No, Sebastian. I actually quit. I'm married now and have a family I would do anything to protect."

"Why didn't you tell me?"

"Because I didn't want you to bring me on BLACK Security out of some kind of kindhearted move on your part. I wanted to earn my seat at the table."

"You've more than earned it, sweetheart." The tension in his hold eases and his expression softens. "Are you sure this is what you want?"

I give him a "duh" look. "I asked to join BLACK Security a while back, remember? But fair warning, I will be suggesting some changes, starting with: *Holy cow, can we please change the deadbolt on your office door to a manual one?*"

Nodding his agreement, a pleased smile spreads across my husband's handsome face as he gathers me in his arms once more. "We're going to make one hell of an unstoppable team, Little Red."

"I wholeheartedly agree, Mister Black."

We both look down at his pants' pocket when his phone pings with an incoming text. "Who would be texting you this late?"

Retrieving his phone, Sebastian sends a quick response, then slips it back into his pocket. "That was Mina saying thank you for catching Isabel's killers."

My chest feels like it's sinking. "I'm sorry she didn't call to say that, Sebastian."

"She called me earlier today."

"She did?" My heart rate jumps right back up. "What did she say?"

"She told me she understood my decision and asked if we could watch Josi overnight and on the day of the funeral, because she's already feeling overwhelmed with all the preparations."

I release a soft breath, so happy that Mina came around. "You told her we would, right?"

"Of course." He leans close and kisses the tip of my nose. "You truly are a quiet storm."

"Huh?"

"Just something my dad said about you," he says, cupping my face. "Thank you for bringing my sister back into our lives, Talia. I never could've told her the truth about her mom."

"You really didn't think I was letting stubborn Blake genes interfere with our goddaughter time, did you?"

Sebastian snorts and quickly sweeps me up into his arms. "Off to bed with you, Little Red." As he carries me through the doorway to our bedroom, he says, "So about my ring...how wide is the band?"

"Sebastian!" I laugh at his persistence and kiss his jaw, whispering into his ear, "Your ring is covered in red fur with black trim, for your comfort of course."

CHAPTER TWENTY-ONE

Sebastian

I haven't seen my wife in twenty-six hours and as I arrive at the church to marry her again in front of our family and friends, I'm tense as hell. The Blake family buried Isabel two weeks before, and now that my wedding day has arrived, I feel like I'm being kicked in the balls as I walk up the church steps once more.

Talia and I purposely set our wedding to be during the brightest part of the day and with the least amount of traffic, but I can't stop scanning for threats, looking for anyone lurking: a car that's idling too long or turned at a strange angle, a man dropping a bag in the street or a woman biking past. My fists clench and my jaw tightens with worry that someone will try to harm the woman I would lay down my life for.

"Honest to God, Sebastian. I wish you drank, because you need a shot or ten of something that would knock you on your ass," Calder says as he takes the steps two at a time to keep up with my fast pace. "We've got everything covered. No one is going to fuck up your wedding day."

I turn at the top of the stairs and scan for the extra security I've hired to fill the streets around the church, both obvious security wearing tuxes as well as men in plain clothes out jogging, taking a dog for a walk, or reading a book on a bench. We had a brief issue with three men who seemed to be hanging around more than they should, but after my guys got involved, it turned out that Adam had sent some plain clothes guards of his own too. Once I reassigned those men to the reception hotel, where there are more vulnerable access points to cover, we're now back on track.

Talia made me promise I wouldn't try to see her in her dress before she walked down the aisle. She'd spent last night with Cass at their old apartment and I still haven't heard from Theo yet. "Report in, Theo. Where the hell is my wife?"

My ear bud crackles and his voice comes through. "They arrived with Den at the church twenty minutes ago, Boss. Now go marry our most valued member of BLACK Security. We've got this."

"Thanks," I say, inhaling deeply now that she's safe in the church.

"It's time to go in." Calder buttons his tux as limos begin to pull up outside. Despite his calm comments, he's staring at everyone, his gaze hyper-focused. I appreciate his diligence. He wants this to go as smoothly as I do.

Family members are already standing in the church's entryway. With everyone attending in formal gowns and tuxes, there's an air of heightened excitement and anticipation in their expressions as they all turn when Calder and I enter.

Damien swaggers up and claps me on the shoulder. "You must be doing something right if she agreed to marry your sorry ass again, old man."

"You're never letting that one go, are you?" I mutter as I switch off my earpiece.

Dark eyebrows hiked, his brown eyes flash with cocky amusement. "Nope. Soaking it up for all it's worth, big brother."

That's the first time Damien has called me "brother" without snark. I hide my surprise behind a low chuckle. "That's only because you've never grown up."

"Why should I? It's overrated."

Gavin is standing just behind him, his expression stoic. We haven't spoken since our encounter in our father's office. The last thing I want is a confrontation, but he's here, so Mina must've worked some of her magic.

When I nod to acknowledge his presence, Gavin slides his hands in his pockets and tilts his head to the side, indicating he wants to talk.

While Damien turns to Calder to chat about the reception afterward, I move away from the crowd to meet my resentful brother. "Whatever it is, Gavin. Today is not the day you want to go head-to-head with me."

"You mustn't *ever* tell him, Sebastian. I'll do whatever it takes for you to keep it between us. He feels guilty enough about you and the past. If he learned about our mother's betrayal…as strong as he is, something like that could devastate him."

"I have no intention of telling Adam, Gavin. Family always comes first for me. I thought you would've figured that out by now."

The tension in his face eases. "Damien might hide his pain and regret behind humor and snark, but that's not how I operate. Nothing can excuse what she did to you and your mom. All I can do is try to make it right." He glances toward our father shaking hands with guests starting to arrive. "The CEO position is yours if you want it."

I put my hand on Gavin's shoulder, drawing his attention back to me. "What I *want* is for you to show our father what a kickass CEO looks like. If you need my help in any way, you've got it."

Gavin's bowtie bobs with his swallow as he nods, his shoulders relaxing. "You didn't owe me that, so thanks. I'll try to live up to the expectation."

Releasing him, my gaze sharpens. "See that you do.

One fourth of that company is mine, little brother."

"I'm not sure that five months age difference counts," he says, eyebrow elevated.

"Even one minute counts. Best you remember that," I say just as Mina walks up in a dark floor length gown. Josi is on her hip in a floral dress and shiny patent shoes.

"Look how handsome you two are." Mina eyes Gavin and me with a wide smile. "Makes me wish I'd brought my phone for a pic instead of leaving it in the car."

"I've got mine," Damien says as he and Calder walk up.

"Of course you do."

I smirk at Gavin's deadpan comment as Damien hands his phone to Calder, then waves us closer. "Come on, let's grab a quick family shot before the photographer makes us stand in a gazillion different poses after the wedding."

With Gavin and Damien flanking either side, Mina slides in between Damien and me. "Make room for the girls, boys," she huffs, wrapping her arm around my waist. Smiling, I drop my arm around her and include Josi's tiny shoulder too, pulling them close to my side.

"Ready?" Calder says, holding the phone up.

He snaps five photos in rapid succession before any of us have even looked his way. "Calder..." Mina fusses, "Do a count!"

"Fine. One, two, say...'Calder's the best!'"

"Calder's an ass." Damien flashes a toothy grin,

making us all laugh.

Of course that's the shot Calder takes.

"I give up." Mina sighs, then turns to look at me as the guys check out the pictures. She hasn't released her hold on my waist, so I smile down at my little sister and niece, thankful we've worked out our issues. "Thank you, Seb," she says, her brown gaze misting. "From the bottom of my heart. Thank you."

"I wish your time with her could've been longer," I say, but she quickly shakes her head, blonde curls swinging.

"No, I'm thanking you for being my brother so many times over. I can't begin to tell you how much it means to me and Josi."

"You're welcome, but your thanks aren't necessary." I release her and tickle Josi's belly until she bursts into giggles. "You're my sister. End of story."

Mina laughs along with Josi, then sobers. "You truly are the best, Seb. I'm happy you found someone who's equally as worthy."

The doors begin to open to the church and an older woman in a stately gown walks through, announcing, "Everyone, if you wouldn't mind taking your seats. The ceremony will begin in ten minutes."

Movement in my periphery draws my attention. Cass is waving from a side door on the left. She's staring directly at me with an intense, no-nonsense look on her face. "Ahem, it's *tradition* to already be in your places, wedding party peeps."

I shoot Calder a look of triumph as she disappears behind the door. He shakes his head in a fast jerk. "Doesn't count. Not about our wedding."

"Technically, there's still plenty of time."

Calder flashes an assured smile. "I'll measure your office while you're on your honeymoon. You know, so I can be ready to move in."

"Move in? What are you two talking about?"

"Nothing," Calder and I say in unison.

Smiling at Mina, I say, "See you up front."

My sister waves and hands Josi off to Adam before heading for the door Cass came through.

Adam settles Josi on his hip and nods to me before walking inside the church with his granddaughter. The silent exchange felt strangely personal. With just a look, I knew what he was saying. *You're welcome for the extra men. Keep her safe and happy. We'll talk later. BLACK Security owes me a contract.* My father and I are starting to get each other more and more.

Right behind my father, I see Talia's aunt walk into the church with her favorite foodie friend and sidekick, Charlie. I'm glad he's with her. The guy seems to have a sensible head.

I pass Talia's father on my way to the side door on the right. He's saying goodbye to a blonde woman who appears to be a dozen years his junior. "I'll meet you up front in just a little bit, Simone."

As she walks into the church, he holds his hand out to me. "Well, Sebastian...it's almost that time."

I clasp his hand with a firm grip. "Thank you for being here for Talia, Kenneth. It means a lot."

He shakes my hand, a wide smile on his face. "It's a wonderful opportunity for a father to give his daughter in marriage to a man he already knows loves her unconditionally."

I smile. "Can't argue with you there."

I move to release his hand, but he tightens his grip. "I would tell you to take care of my girl, but you've proven you're more than capable. May you have the kind of marriage I wish I'd had...long-lived and well-loved."

"Thanks, Kenneth."

Releasing my hand, he heads for the door on the left.

I wait until he closes the door behind him and one of my guards steps in front of it before I open the door on the right to make my way to the front of the church.

I've impatiently waited through one song for the bridesmaids and groomsmen to take their places, and I'm pretty sure I've ground through the top layer of enamel on my back teeth while listening for the wedding march to start.

When the organ sounds echo up to the rafters and the

church doors slowly swing open, I almost fall to my knees at the beautiful sight Talia makes standing up front with her father.

As they proceed forward and Den closes the door behind them, standing guard the moment it's shut, the crowd buzzes with titters and awed appreciation for Talia's break from tradition with her wedding attire. While more than a few ladies quietly clap as she passes, the lump in my throat grows bigger.

She's wearing an off-the-shoulder, mermaid-style wedding gown in white that forms to her curves, but my adoring wife has also incorporated a bold red sash across her small waist.

With each step she takes, I can see the rounded edges of the big bow tied at her back and my throat starts to itch and my eyes burn.

I don't know how the woman always surprises and humbles me at the same time, but she's done it in such a deeply personal way that I'm so fucking glad the aisle is long and the song is slow because I'm going to need the time to get my emotions in check.

Talia finally reaches me as the music ends, and once Kenneth kisses her on the cheek and takes his seat, I take her hand to help her stand in front of me.

Before Pastor Meyer starts to speak, Talia curls her finger for me to bend close.

I lean forward, thinking she's going to break tradition

yet again and kiss me, but she plucks the earpiece from my ear and turns it on and speaks into it, loud enough for our family and friends to hear. "Love you guys. See you at the reception." When she turns it off and drops the piece into my coat pocket, then pats it with a determined smile, the entire congregation uproars with laughter. While the pastor raises his arms to get them to settle down, Talia whispers, "This color is called *red wine*."

"May I continue now, Talia?" Pastor Meyer says.

As she nods for him to proceed, I'm floored yet again that the sash she's wearing is the one from our table-top wine tasting session. Her sparkling eyes shift back to me and I enjoy the hell out of her secret smile, returning it in kind.

"Sebastian and Talia are already married, but they wanted to reaffirm their vows here and now with their loved ones present, since family and friends are important in their daily lives." The pastor turns to me. "You may begin, Sebastian."

I take Talia's hands in mine and lift them to kiss the ring on her finger, speaking so everyone can hear. "When I gave Talia this ring, I never wanted her to remove it, which is why she's still wearing it today. I told her then that I would love and protect her, but never smother her, and I chose a ring with a moving center band that represented my promise to be together but independent."

Talia's eyes mist a little as I speak.

"Talia, you're always thoughtfully bold and I'm forever in awe of your ability to be compassionate no matter the circumstance. You are the one who keeps me in check *and* balanced in both life and love, the person who has made me a better husband, brother, and son.

"Since you already have your ring, I had a wedding gift all planned, but recent circumstances gave me an opportunity for a present that I hope will have an even deeper meaning."

I reach in my coat pocket. Lifting my hand up, I dangle an updated version of her Two Lias heart locket. Talia gasps and captures the spinning heart. Her eyes glitter with tears of happiness as she stares at the tiny red and black diamond encrusted centers of the two hearts on the front of the locket. "It's perfect, Sebastian."

Smiling, I clasp it around her neck.

When she lifts her happy gaze to mine, my heart feels full. "Your ring might mean together but independent, Little Red, but since we've been together, I have learned that I am dependent on you for my happiness. There is no independent for me, not anymore."

Talia's lips tremble, but she can't hold back her tears. As I smile at her and gently thumb the wetness away, the pastor smiles and looks at her. "Your turn, Talia."

Talia nods and sniffs as she takes my hands in hers. I can feel her shaking, so I squeeze her hands to encourage her.

"You are the bravest man with the biggest heart, Sebastian. I love every stubborn, bull-headed, never-quit, hard-working, family-loving part of you." She glances down at her ring then back to me. "I don't know if you noticed but the red diamond center band on my ring doesn't spin any more."

When I frown, she shakes her head. "I could've had it fixed, but I felt it was appropriate. See, at first the band spun freely, later it turned much slower, then it took real effort to get it to move at all, and I realized that my ring is following our love. I'm no longer able to see my life without you in it, nor do I want to. We're stuck together. You are the center of my happiness, Sebastian."

Talia has never spoken so deeply about her feelings before and it's hard for me not to let my emotions cloud my vision. Thankfully she saves me from making a complete wuss of myself when she dips her fingers into the folds of her red sash and pulls my ring out.

"Finally," I mutter as she slides it on my finger.

Talia addresses our loved ones watching from the pews. "Yeah, *finally*. This man's been going around without a ring for way too long!"

While laughter echoes throughout the church and among the wedding party, she looks at me. "Now you'll never be without color in your life."

Very few family and friends know the true meaning behind her comment, but I'm so moved by her sentiment, I glance down at the ring. When all I see is black, frustration rises over my colorblindness, but I tamp it down and lift my gaze to hers.

Talia's smile is so heartfelt as she continues to hold the ring on my finger. "But even then, Sebastian, you'll have to know where to look."

She glances down once more and I follow her gaze. My loving wife slowly spins my ring around until I see what looks like a sunrise against a dark sky across the side of the band. I can see the striation of gray scale color changes, and then once the colors move into the red spectrum... those colors I can see, but the romantic memories a sunrise evokes are priceless.

When she lifts my hand and kisses the ring, I'm fucking done. A tear escapes before I can hold it back.

Everyone begins to clap, but the pastor raises his hands to shush them.

Once they quiet, Talia takes my hands in hers. "I love you, Sebastian Quinn Blake. I'm honored to be your wife and so happy to have another chance to stand up in front of friends and family and promise to always love you and keep you in our hearts and minds."

While Talia holds my gaze, my brain stutters over her binding vow.

Just as I give her a questioning look, she lowers my ring hand to her belly and repeats, "Keep you in *our* hearts and minds."

Holy fuck! "Are you serious?" My heart skips a beat and I quickly clasp her face, not caring one whit that a couple more tears escape.

When Talia wraps her fingers around my wrists and nods, the cheers and claps spread around the room to the shocked, but happy relatives in our wedding party, and then even to our stoic pastor, who throws his hands up and grins wide, joining everyone else in celebrating the news.

With the sound in the room rising to near-deafening level as people begin to stand in front of their pews, I pull my wife close and press my nose to hers, my hands shaking with elation. "You never cease to shock the hell out of me, Little Red. God, I fucking love you."

CHAPTER TWENTY-TWO

Talia

"Do you think Cass will forgive me for keeping this a secret?" I say as we step into our bedroom. I'm not surprised Sebastian didn't want to stay at the reception partying all night long, but I am a little surprised he brought us home to our apartment instead of the lush hotel Cass had booked for us. "It's just that I did spend all last night with Cass having fun girl talk about all kinds of things. And she did help plan my wedding as well as help me get dressed for the wedding and—"

"The question you should be asking is: 'Would Sebastian forgive me if I told Cass about my pregnancy before him?'" He shrugs out of his tux jacket and pulls his bowtie, unhooking his top collar button before sitting down on our bed. "And the answer is most definitely 'no'.

Your husband wouldn't have forgiven you if you had told Cass before him."

"But you're okay that you learned at the same time as everyone else?" I ask, my voice a quiet hush. I know I took a big gamble, but I wouldn't be able to keep it a secret for much longer. My breasts were already getting bigger. "I mean, I know how much you hate the anticipation of surprises—"

"Talia..." Sebastian pulls me onto his lap, resting his hand on my thigh. "I'm not angry or upset. The reason I brought you here instead of to the hotel before we fly out tomorrow on our honeymoon is sheer selfishness. I want to spend a night with you all to myself and in our own bed as the newly minted, family-approved Mr. and Mrs. Blake."

I touch his ring, running my fingers over it. "But you wished I had told you alone?"

He lifts my chin and makes me meet his gaze. "You made this day a memory I'll never forget. And for that, I love you..." He lowers his hand to my belly. "And our baby. I'm thrilled, proud, and so fucking happy right now. Your aunt and father seemed very excited about the baby at the reception, probably more so than the wedding."

"Yes, they were happy," I say, nodding. "And how about him bringing Simone as his plus one."

"Who is she?"

"She's the new girl he hired to help out with his ads

and with other stuff in the bookstore."

"Well more power to him," he says chuckling.

I shrug. "It was just surprising for sure."

He flexes his hand on my stomach. "Speaking of surprises...how far along are you?"

"Almost eight weeks."

When his brow shadows, I press my lips to it and whisper, "I waited for an appointment with the doctor I really wanted."

He scowls. "No OB/GYN should make you wait that long to be seen."

"It wasn't his fault. The home pregnancy tests were wonky so I waited until they seemed consistent. You don't want to know how many I went through."

"Is everything okay?"

"Everything is perfect. My levels are right where they should be."

"All the little things...You falling asleep early, eating extra pieces of pizza—" His eyes light up with clarity. "—you getting me to drink your wine...now it's all suddenly falling into place."

"I don't even want to talk about the bouts of queasy stomach," I say wryly. "As for the wine, you do know that was more about getting you to relax, right?"

"I definitely got the *relaxing* part," he says, flashing a grin. "About your doctor appointments, you're not going to any more without me. I want to see the little noodle."

Laughing, I rest my hand over his. "Noodle? What is it with you and food nicknames?"

"It's Noodle until I see for myself and inspiration strikes."

When I smile at the idea of him seeing our baby for the first time, his gaze drops to his hand on my stomach. I lift his hand and turn his ring until we can see the sunset. "Do you like your ring?"

"To say that I don't think you'll ever be able to top everything you did to make today extra special is an understatement, sweetheart."

His broad smile makes all the trouble I went through getting his ring made, having the sash added to my dress and waiting to announce my pregnancy all worth it. "I wanted your ring to be in the best metal, so I chose platinum, but I also wanted it to be black. I did some research and found a college that's using cutting edge technology with a tabletop laser to change the color of metals."

He stares at my ring, intrigued. "So that's not painted?"

"No, all those colors are part of your ring. A breathtaking sunrise is forever etched in your band, Mister Black—"

His lips cut me off, but I don't mind his sudden kiss one bit. Instead, I lean into his hard chest and welcome the enticing taste of his lips and tongue sliding along mine in a slow, deep exploration.

"I love kissing you," he murmurs against my mouth, his hand sliding into my pinned up hair to pull me closer.

"We can just do this all night if you want," I tease against the corner of his mouth.

His hand fists in my hair and he nips at my bottom lip. "Hell no, I'm just getting started."

I cup his jaw and bite his bottom lip back, loving my husband so much my heart feels it might burst right out of my form-fitted dress.

My skin prickles when he tugs my dress's zipper down. He pauses when he reaches the zipper's end, his voice a rough rumble. "Unless you want your wedding dress in tatters, I suggest you step out of it and hang it up, Little Red."

As Sebastian walks into our closet, unbuttoning his shirt, I kick off my heels and wiggle out of my dress, laying it across the back of a side chair.

Wearing nothing but a G-string and garters, I walk over to the Two Lias picture on the tall dresser and stare at it as I take off my necklace. "I hope I'm a good mom." My lip crooks in a half smile. "At least Sebastian isn't afraid to change a diaper. There's always that." But the fact my husband is so good with Josi settles my worries. Sebastian will be there for me. He'll help me get through any baby blues I might have after our child is born. I can only hope I'm not affected that way, but with my mom's history, it's still in the back of my mind. "You'll watch over us, right, Amelia?" I whisper as I start to drape the necklace along the corner of the picture.

"You don't have to take it off," my husband says from right behind me. I immediately tense.

"How do you manage to get so close without me noticing?"

"Trade secret." He chuckles as he leans close, the heat of his bare chest warming my back. "This version is waterproof, so you can wear it in the shower if you like."

I open the locket and smile at the picture of Josi and me and then the Two Lias drawing. Closing the locket, I run my finger over the red diamond heart and then the black one. I pull it closer when I realize one heart slightly overlaps the other and where they overlap…the stones are a mixture of red and black. God, this man just melts my heart. "Aww, the blending of the two hearts is just perfect! This is truly gorgeous and so incredibly thoughtful, Sebastian. Thank you."

He rests his chin on my shoulder, his arms encircling my waist. "There's one more change I made to the original necklace. Do you see it?"

I flip the locket over and don't see anything on the back, but when I start to turn it back, I see another lip on the edge of the locket and press my fingernail inside it.

When the back pops open to reveal two empty picture slots, I whisper, "Did you know?" and blink to keep from tearing up. These pregnancy hormones are really kicking my emotions into high gear.

Sebastian kisses my neck, his hands sliding along my

waist. "No. I had the back panel added in the hopes that one day we would fill it with our own children's pictures too."

Taking it from my shaking hands, he hooks the necklace around my neck once more, then slides his hands slowly along my shoulders and down across my breasts. Moving one hand below my breast, he flattens the other on my belly. "I love you, Talia. Thank you for sharing your life with me and trusting me with your heart. I promise to always protect it."

I squeeze my eyes shut and take a deep breath. I know part of my extreme emotions are hormonal, but I love this man so much. That will never change. Lifting my arms over my head, I drape them around his neck and pull him even closer. "Right now my heart doesn't need protecting…it needs revving. Do you know anyone who can help me with that?"

With a low rumble, he slides a warm hand along my thigh until he reaches my ass and gives it a firm slap. "How hot do you want it, Little Red?"

As he rubs my ass cheek, then grips it with a possessive hold, my sex tightens and throbs, soaking through my G-string. I spear my fingers in his hair and grab on tight, pulling to get his full attention. "I'd like fire engine red, please."

I gasp when he dips his fingers into my body, sliding them along and around the G-string. "You're sopping and so fucking warm," he growls, pressing his erection against me as he delivers an even harder smack.

I don't miss that each time he lights my body on fire with the sensual sting of his palm, his other hand flattens protectively on my belly. I'm both touched and aroused by the realization, but I also want him to let go, so I put one hand on the dresser for support and arch my back, wantonly pressing my ass against him. "Then do something about it. This fire isn't going out without your help."

Sebastian hooks his thumb on my G-string and shreds the flimsy lace with a flick of his wrist. His breathing ramps and just when I think he's going to slide inside me from behind, he quickly turns me around and lifts me up. The moment the tip of his cock touches my pussy, he shakes his head and his is voice a desperate rasp, "Can't wait, Talia."

As soon as my back hits the dresser, I hook my legs around his body and yank him close.

"Is a raw, rough fuck what you want, Little Red?" he says, his warm breath bathing my shoulder while he stays just outside of my body, teasing me.

Panting, I claw at his muscular shoulders to let him know what I want.

He dips just inside me and exhales a harsh groan. "I want to hear the words."

"Raw, Rough. Hard. Soft. Just fuck me, Sebastian!"

A primal grunt of male satisfaction rumbles from his

chest as he slams into me. I gasp my pleasure and clasp him close, rolling my hips and seeking release from the pent-up arousal building between us.

Pulling back, he jerks his hips forward and stays buried deep, applying pressure against my clit. My heart stutters as an orgasm spirals through my body in bone-melting pulses of erotic pleasure.

I clench against him and whisper in his ear, "This is just round one," right before I bite down on his shoulder.

Sebastian lets out a feral groan and captures my lips in a dominant kiss as he thrusts once more, pulsing deep inside me.

Clasping my ass in a firm hold, he carries us to the bed and chuckles when I lay my head on his shoulder and murmur, "Did I mention the rounds would be between naps?"

"That's a promise I'm holding you to, Little Red."

CHAPTER TWENTY-THREE

Sebastian

"I'm here," Den says quietly as he steps off the penthouse elevator and moves to stand beside me by the window.

We wait in silence for the sunrise. As the soft rays begin to peak over the horizon, I fold my arms at my back. "You know, I honestly don't believe there's such a thing as coincidence..." I cut my gaze his way. "Like your MI6 buddy suddenly coming to Manhattan looking for work right when it became apparent Talia needed her own bodyguard."

Den turns to face me, eyebrow hiked. "Since when has Talia *not* needed a full time guard?"

"I'll give you the touché but not the pass." When he doesn't say anything, I continue, my tone drilling, "I'm also fucking *excellent* with timelines..."

Den turns toward the glass once more. Inhaling deeply, he closes his eyes against the morning sun. "I called Alexander and asked him to come interview with Adam the day after the bomb went off."

"We didn't know the bomb was meant for Talia at that point," I say, my tension growing. "Did you know about her pregnancy?"

His eyes open and he unbuttons his jacket to slip his hands into his pockets. "Her pregnancy solidified my decision, yes." He dips his head. "Congratulations, by the way."

The question festers in my mind. I start to speak, but Den cuts me off.

"And before you ask if she told me, she didn't. The moment the bomb went off, her hand went straight to her stomach. It's a reflexive thing, a mother's instinct. She didn't even know she did it."

Hearing the truth eases the tightness in my chest; I'm more than thankful he stepped up. I clear my throat and nod. "Thank you for watching over her. She's—"

"An inherently good person. There aren't enough of them in the world." He glances my way. "That's why they need people like us."

An unspoken agreement passes between us before he looks down at his watch. "You have to be at the airport in two hours."

"Thanks for coming. I know you were supposed to

have today off."

"I wasn't going to let your driver take you to the airport anyway."

"Our driver is highly trained, Den."

"Not like me, he's not," he counters.

He's got me there. I rub my chin, eyeing him. "In a battle of the best overall, I wonder who would win, a SEAL or an MI6 agent?"

He cracks a confident smile, then shrugs. "Your honeymoon should start the moment you leave this building, Sebastian."

"Point taken. I shouldn't be more than an hour." With a curt nod, I pick up the folder from the table and head for the elevator.

My phone rings as I exit the elevator on the top floor of Blake Towers. "Blake."

"I'm in house cleaning mode and I need some info," Banks's deep voice rumbles in my ear.

"Why haven't you lost my number already?" I snap, tucking the folder under my arm.

"Blackie, *Blackie.* I'm a bit hurt. I thought we'd bonded through our ordeal."

"What do you want, Banks?"

"Just following up now that you've tied the knot. Talia mentioned that she tried to give me a heads up, so that means someone else at the Tribune ratted me out to the police. You don't happen to know who that was, do you?"

I promised Talia I'd let her handle her affairs at the Tribune, because I didn't want to put her job at risk, but now that she's no longer there, this scenario works for me.

"You're far smarter than you look, Banks. Do the math. It wasn't my wife, nor was it her guard."

"You mean it was that annoying, curly haired guy?"

Though Nathan deserves a good pounding for putting my wife and child at risk the way he did, I know firsthand just how hard Banks can hit. "You *did* have a stolen painting on your wall, Banks. Make sure any punishment you dole out takes that into account."

"You going soft, Blackie?"

"You tell me? How's your nose?"

"Fucked up. You still owe me a check."

"I just paid it with information." Hanging up, I pull the door open to the executive suite and walk through the empty admin's area to my father's office.

"As promised, my BLACK Security contract," I say, handing my father the folder.

"You're an early bird this morning." Standing, he walks around his desk and sits in the matching leather seat opposite me. "You didn't have to bring it personally. You could've emailed it."

I gesture to the folder. "You should read over it."

"Right now?"

When I nod, he starts to open the folder, then pauses,

his blue eyes full of excitement. "Congratulations on an amazing wedding and baby announcement. I'm beyond thrilled, Sebastian. Being a grandparent...is wonderful."

"As opposed to being a parent?" I smirk that he's talking as if I'd spent my early years with him.

"No, no...grandparents get all the fun and none of the responsibility." He shakes his head, then sighs. "I know I missed your childhood, but I hope it's okay to talk to you about being a parent. I do know a thing or two about being one."

Shaking my head, I smile, strangely not angry like I usually am when the subject of my past comes up. "It's fine. Have a look at the agreement and see if it'll work for you."

Adam opens the folder and skims through it. "Seems fairly straight forward," he says as he turns the last page. Moving the papers, he lifts another set, his brow furrowed. "This is an investment contract."

"It is."

His blue eyes lift to mine. "But you said you didn't want me to be involved."

"No, I said I didn't want you to buy me out. I want to expand my business to the corporate sector and for that I'll need an investor."

He flips through the pages once more. "This is impressive, Sebastian. I can see so much potential in the corporate world. The need for security on every level is growing by leaps and bounds. Even the international markets could be an option."

I chuckle that he's already thinking ahead. "Talia said the same thing. This expansion is her idea."

"I'm not surprised at all. I'm all for this. How soon would you start taking on corporate clients?"

"Whoa." I hold my hands up. "We're not expanding yet. I want to use Blake Industries as a training ground for my employees. We'll get all the kinks out and start the expansion after that, but first we need to learn what value we can bring and where."

My father snaps the folder shut, his eye shining. "Not that I wish your honeymoon time away, but I can't wait to get started on this."

I stand and button my suit jacket, holding out my hand to him. As my father clasps my hand, I say, "Read over the fine print and send over any changes. We'll hammer out any negotiable sticking points once I get back."

"Will do. Have a wonderful time with Talia, son. You both deserve it."

As I pull my car out onto the road, I smile thinking about Talia. And our baby. I can't believe I'm going to be a father. I feel like opening the top of my sports car and shouting the news to the whole world. Knowing how she felt and why she didn't tell me about her job, I think it was for the best that I didn't know about her job situation before I asked her to come work with me at BLACK Security. But, holy shit, am I'm glad that I didn't know about the baby beforehand, or she'd never believe that my offer for her to work at BLACK Security wasn't just some machination on my part to get her out of a dangerous job and under my protective wing.

Would I have done just that? Hell yes, truth be told. I would have done whatever it took to get her out of that job, but at least this way…we won't have that as an issue between us. I want my family surrounded by people who only care about their well-being and that's exactly what Talia and our child will get.

And I think she knows she's truly an asset at BLACK Security. With a mind like hers and mine working together…the sky's the limit.

My phone buzzes and when I press the speaker, Talia's out-of-breath voice pops through. "Where are you?"

"I'm on my way back," I say, my whole body tensing. "Is everything okay?"

"We're leaving in twenty minutes and I just realized I don't have any sunscreen. A redhead in the Mediterranean without sunscreen? I might spontaneously combust the moment I get off the plane. *Argh*, what was I thinking?"

Here's a woman who outsmarted and trapped a mastermind homicidal cop, and who took down a backstabbing kidnapper, but she's freaking out over a bottle of sunscreen?

"What are you laughing at? Is the idea of me going *poof*

that amusing?"

I didn't even realize I was laughing. "I'm sorry," I say, sobering. "I'll grab some sunscreen on my way back."

"Whew, okay, crisis averted. Now where are my sunglasses? My bathing suit is already packed, and I've got three notebooks and plenty of pens—"

"Talia?"

"Yes?"

"We're going to have a great time."

"I know we will."

"You know why?"

"Because you're picking up my sunscreen?"

"Because we'll be together, Little Red...and that's all that matters. Just you and me..."

She takes a deep breath and sings-songs, "And little noodle too."

I bark out a laugh. "And little noodle too."

Hanging up, I punch on the gas, a wide smile on my face.

God, I really do fucking love that woman.

Stay tuned for REDDEST BLACK (IN THE SHADOWS, Book 7)!

If you found **BLACK PLATINUM** an entertaining and enjoyable read, I hope you'll consider taking the time to leave a review and share your thoughts in the online bookstore where you purchased it. Your review could be the one to help another reader decide to read BLACK PLATINUM and the other books in the IN THE SHADOWS series!

To be informed when **REDDEST BLACK** releases, join my free newsletter http://bit.ly/11tqAQN. An email will come to your inbox on the day a new book releases.

Other Books by
P.T. MICHELLE

In the Shadows Series (Contemporary Romance, 18+)
Mister Black (Part 1 - Talia and Sebastian)
Scarlett Red (Part 2 - Talia and Sebastian)
Blackest Red (Part 3 - Talia and Sebastian)
Gold Shimmer (Book 4 - Cass and Calder)
Steel Rush (Book 5 - Cass and Calder)
Black Platinum (Book 6 - Talia and Sebastian)
Reddest Black (Book 7 – Talia and Sebastian) – Late Fall 2017

Brightest Kind of Darkness Series
(YA/New Adult Paranormal Romance, 16+)
Ethan (Prequel)
Brightest Kind of Darkness (book 1)
Lucid (book 2)
Destiny (book 3)
Desire (book 4)
Awaken (book 5)

To contact P.T. Michelle and stay up-to-date on her latest releases:

WEBSITE
http://www.ptmichelle.com

FACEBOOK
https://www.facebook.com/PTMichelleAuthor

TWITTER
https://twitter.com/P.T.Michelle

INSTAGRAM
http://instagram.com/p.t.michelle/

GOODREADS
https://www.goodreads.com/author/
show/4862274.P_T_Michelle

PINTEREST
http://www.pinterest.com/ptmichelle/

Sign up/join P.T. Michelle's:

NEWSLETTER
(free newsletter announcing book releases and
special contests)
http://bit.ly/11tqAQN

FACEBOOK READERS' GROUP
https://www.facebook.com/groups/376324052499720/

ACKNOWLEDGEMENTS

To my amazing beta readers: Joey Berube and Amy Bensette, thank you for your ability to not only read quickly, but to also provide invaluable feedback, not just as fans of my books, but also with the desire to make the book the best it can be. I appreciate your thoughtful inputs that helped make BLACK PLATINUM a truly fantastic read.

To my wonderful critique partner, Trisha Wolfe, thank you for reading *Black Platinum* so quickly, for your insights and for the brainstorming sessions! Our Google searches… haha! Big hugs!

To my family, thank you for understanding the time and effort each book takes. I love you all and truly appreciate your unending support. And to my husband for reading BLACK PLATINUM and requesting that I add a chapter, thank you.

To my fabulous fans, I can't thank you enough for your love of my IN THE SHADOWS series and characters! Thank you so much for spreading the word by posting reviews and telling all your reader friends about the series whenever you get a chance. Thank you for all the fantastic support! It means the world to me!

ABOUT THE AUTHOR

P.T. Michelle is the *NEW YORK TIMES*, *USA TODAY*, and International Bestselling author of the contemporary romance series IN THE SHADOWS, the YA/New Adult crossover series BRIGHTEST KIND OF DARKNESS, and the romance series: BAD IN BOOTS, KENDRIAN VAMPIRES and SCIONS (listed under Patrice Michelle). She keeps a spiral notepad with her at all times, even on her nightstand. When P.T. isn't writing, she can usually be found reading or taking pictures of landscapes, sunsets and anything beautiful or odd in nature.

To keep up-to-date when the next
P.T. Michelle book will release,
join P.T.'s free newsletter http://bit.ly/11tqAQN

66883007R10176

Made in the USA
Lexington, KY
27 August 2017